The Butcher of the Forest

T0005627

ALSO BY PREMEE MOHAMED

THE BUTCHER OF THE FOREST

PREMEE MOHAMED

TOR PUBLISHING GROUP

NEW YORK

THE BUTCHER OF THE FOREST

Cover art and design by Andrew Davis

A Tordotcom Book
Published by Tom Doherty Associates / Tor Publishing Group
120 Broadway
New York, NY 10271

www.tor.com

Tor® is a registered trademark of Macmillan Publishing Group, LLC.

ISBN 978-1-250-88178-6 (trade paperback)
ISBN 978-1-250-88179-3 (ebook)

First Edition: 2024

For my brother

The Butcher of the Forest

It was not yet dawn when they came for her.

Veris stumbled from her bed into an early-morning sea, deep blue light submerging the little house with no hint of sun; she swam, it seemed, to the lamp in the hall, and lit it with a wavery half-smothered match; she swam down the stairs.

The front door rattled in its frame with each blow, paint and shreds of wood flaking from it, as if the unseen callers were not knocking but rushing at it with a battering ram. It was locked from the inside, but the bolts and bars were beginning to give as she approached. She unlocked it hastily, cursing and fumbling the ancient keys, and threw it wide.

"This the residence of Veris Thorn?" The man on the doorstep still raised his gauntleted fist, as if, the door now conquered, he would hammer her as well for a wrong or slothful answer.

"I am she."

"Then get in."

She opened her mouth to ask for clarification, then

looked past his shoulder (also armored, she noted numbly). A carriage waited at the end of the path. It had clearly arrived in such haste that in stopping it had slewed into their garden wall; the newly exposed faces of stone frowned and palely glowed. Two more armed men flanked its open door, and another sat the reins, leaning forward as if already in motion. All she could see was the skeletal gleam of starlight on the metal, so that they formed, more or less, attitudes, rather than men.

It took her a moment, but once arrived there was no escaping it: they had come from the Tyrant, and she could no more deny them than she could the rising of the sun. Her stomach sank, and her limbs began to drain of sensation; behind her, adroitly, her aunt took the lamp before it smashed on the doorstep.

"I—" Veris said.

"Now," growled the man, and he took her upper arm, pulling her out of the doorway.

"May I get dressed, at le—"

"No."

Veris glanced back desperately as she was towed away, at her aunt and her grandfather in the amber lamplight, sleepy, confused only, their faces not showing terror, not yet. Receding, receding, till they were no more than silhouettes, and the man slung her smoothly into the carriage so that her slippered feet did not even touch the three steps leading up into it, and then he got in and sat across from her.

The carriage squeaked as the other two men jumped onto the running-boards, and in silence, without clucking to the horses, the driver took them down the lane; and Veris thought only of these men who had come in heavy armor, bristling with swords and daggers, through the village, and how ready they were for violence, and what might have happened if she had for some unfathomable reason not been at the house.

No. Best not to think about it. Veris had no mother, and she had no father, but she had family still to preserve, and she would not jeopardize them now. She shivered in silence in the carriage, knowing that her escorts would not answer any of her questions anyway.

They bounced along the rutted lane, passing all the tiny houses just like hers, still mostly dark, then the dull apple-red glow of the bakery and the dozen ovens, tiny forms already scurrying around in the deep blue light with wheelbarrows and barrels. Then the road rattled with gravel, then cobbles, and they were out of the old town and onto the new way which the Tyrant had paved with flagstones to more easily move his armies. Past the smithies and the tanners, the small golden lights of farmhouses, and the carriage sped up now, a speed she would have called reckless but the Tyrant's carriages ran on steel wheels which would not, like the age-old wooden ones, crack or turn on the road, and his powerful horses had been bred to the task.

The sun edged over the distant hills, only a lightening of the general murk, an aubergine rather than a blue. It illuminated the bridge of the man's nose across from her and nothing else. The carriage's small, leaded windows were propped half-open, presumably for his comfort, but between the autumn air and the speed of their motion, Veris was chilled to the bone. She drew her threadbare robe around her pajamas, for what little good it would do, and watched the land blossom around them: the fields of wheat, barley, the strict grids of orchards, regiments of trellises heavy with grapes.

Best time of the year. Eat everything without guilt. Even this air, cool and fresh, ripe with a year's work well done, you could enjoy. There would be Pig Days in the next three or four weeks, the big bonfires, the cauldrons pinging as they heated up . . . and *what* did the Tyrant want with her? Nothing, nothing. She had been trying to keep her mind away from it, to hold down the panic in the question, but she could control it no longer. What, what on *earth*? *Why*?

Not another wife, surely; he liked them young, and Veris was pushing forty. And fertile, too, because he had only two children, or so it was said. A Tyrant always needed more, and so more working wombs. Not hers.

Not to work at the great castle: everyone in the valley clamored for a position there, and the stewards and quartermasters simply rode down to a fair every now and then and recruited servants by the handful. And anyway, Veris would be equally useless as a maid, a groom, a cook, a valet, a footman, anything, as she would a concubine.

Not to arrest her for treason or conspiracy... well, one never knew, but it didn't seem likely to Veris, who generally kept her head down and did not associate, as far as she knew, with any benighted souls who would dare to plot against their conqueror, because she did not really associate with anybody now. It was true, though, that the arrests were still happening; and for slighter and slighter a cause every time, it seemed. But they would have clapped her in irons the moment she opened the door, if that had been the case (and certainly not sent a carriage).

Why, why? What had she *done*?

Despite the effort at ventilation, the rotted leather stench of her escort's armor was beginning to accumulate; Veris pressed her face to the gap in the window and breathed the cleaner air outside, which admittedly smelled of horse-sweat and road dust. Then a burst of resin, leaf, root, as wet and pure as water splashed on her face: the border of the north woods, rising high and dark, shadowing the still-green pasturelands on the other side of the road.

Gone in an instant as they raced past. She had not realized they were moving so quickly until the woods tore away from them like a flag, and then, in the distance, she spotted the high gray walls of the castle. Her fingers tightened on the windowsill till it creaked under her grip. *Still he has this power over us. And it has not waned one whit since the day he came.*

Why me and why?

~

In the old days, so Veris had been told, the throne room had been an abattoir: corpses spiked and decaying both outside and in, heads suspended on chains from the ceiling like Furrowday lanterns, dripping maggots onto the princes and potentates summoned to pay obeisance to the Tyrant. Now it seemed clean enough, though the wall behind his throne remained closely paved with skulls. Teeth, horns, antlers, and the occasional gold filling sparkled as the rising sun began to fill the room.

The guard brought Veris into this place much as he had taken her out of her own: one hand clamped carelessly around her upper arm, encircling it entirely, unmindful of the sharp edges of his gauntlet digging into her goosepimpled flesh. Ten paces from the throne he yanked sharply downwards, throwing her to her knees. Probably she was meant to lie flat or perform some ritual pose, but he seemed satisfied with her kneeling, and retreated a few steps.

Close enough, Veris noted cynically, to grab her if she tried to run.

She shivered, her teeth chattering; she clamped her jaw shut tightly and looked up at the throne and its occupant, the Tyrant, the man with a thousand names and a thousand cities under his bootheel, he who had for no perceptible reason settled here in their land after grinding it into the dust and stamping his name upon it, bringer of death, lord of war, slaughterer of millions.

The first thing she noted about him was that he was drinking out of a cup made of a skull, and she caught herself just in time to forestall a bray of what she knew would be frankly unwise laughter. Well, who knew, maybe he wasn't a drunk, maybe she too would want a cup of wine at sunrise when he told her why she had been brought here.

No one had told her not to speak unless spoken to, but Veris was a sensible woman, and no one needed to tell her. Yet for all this urgency, snatching her out of the morning's darkness, galloping here at speeds inimical to life and limb, he said nothing. Not to test her, she thought at once, but because he had one of those lumps in his throat that she knew very well: apricot-sized, difficult to swallow past, let alone speak. It might come out in a scream or a sob.

The Tyrant was supposed to be in his early sixties, but he looked younger; mostly this was the effect of his long hair, which was glossy and still very black, and only beginning to gray in much the same way as Veris's, giving it a slaty, gilded effect rather than making itself known. He was tall, rangy, powerful, skin of a milky white even tinged with the bluish color you saw sometimes as milk first hit the pail. The numerous small scars upon his face were also white, and barely visible; he had been lucky in healing. Long thin nose, wide thin mouth, white lips invisible as they touched the bone goblet.

His eyes were exactly as rumored, and they froze Veris in terror the way a ghost story will even if you don't believe in ghosts: golden-brown, even reddish, a shade that should have seemed feline but made her think instead and immediately of some far bigger and more bloodthirsty beast that she had never encountered. And they *burned,* partly with wine, partly as if a match had been lit behind either one. They gave off more light than the gems on his crown.

How many had this beast-eyed man and his followers killed so far? Thousands in their valley alone. Maybe millions all told. Most pertinently, her parents, in the last war that had brought him here. Mother, then father. She would never forget that, should she live to be a hundred. Mother first. Father trying to look after her for weeks. Then him too.

Her heart thudded unevenly in her chest; the room went gray around her. His voice cut through it: "You are Veris Thorn."

"Yes, my Lord," she said automatically. She tried to focus on him again. From the corner of her eye, she spotted servants crouched low and trying to move in silence, kindling a fire in the great hearth set into the other wall. One small reprieve: maybe she'd warm up. There was no glass in any of the windows, and they admitted a bright but chilly sun.

The handful of spectators clustered on either side of his throne were shivering too. He gave no indication of the cold.

"You are the one who went into these curst woods and brought back a child," he said.

"Yes," she said, and her stomach sank. *Oh. Oh no. Oh no, no, no, no, no . . .*

"Alive."

"Yes." *Technically,* she almost said; at any rate now that she knew what he was going to ask of her, it would do him no good to know of the child's fate. She felt hollowed out—*scraped* out, like a knife going in to get every last shred of something inside her. *I can't,* she wanted to say, and knew she would not.

At last he moved, and handed the bone cup to a wan-looking girl who scuttled off with it held aloft as if it were a burning coal. "You are to go into the woods again," he said, "and recover my children."

She had known it was coming; it was not phrased as a request. What burned in his eyes was desperation and that surprised her, somewhat; she had gotten the idea that, like the previous kings of the land, there was no great attachment to the children of the throne except as potential future heirs. You could always, the thinking was, have another child; or you could adopt with equal legitimacy. That was all in the laws, if he cared to obey them, which he didn't.

Veris took a deep breath. The room was warming and her wits were settling, if only a little. "My Lord, when did they go into the woods? The exact hour. If you know it. Please."

"We do not know." He clasped his long hands together, the bones beneath the skin no whiter. "Their absence was discovered this morning when their nurse went to raise them up from bed. I had her questioned—"

And here Veris shuddered again, scratching her knees on the stone: they would have tortured the nurse, of course, fearing that she had betrayed the throne. Arranged for the kidnapping of the children, perhaps. Or even their deaths. But the nurse must have been a local girl, and had given them, in the extremity of her pain, Veris's name, and a scrap of local gossip.

"She said she checked on them at midnight and they were asleep," the Tyrant said slowly. "So, two hours ago was when they were found to be gone. I sent out the dogs."

"The trail grew cold at the edge of the woods?"

"Yes. At the edge." His face reddened with sudden anger. "The dogs would go no further. Even beaten, whipped." His accent in her tongue made the harsh words harsher still, as he clipped consonants, swallowed whole vowels. "And the guards who took the dogs... they also disappeared. Only the dogs came back. All bloody. Like meat. Afraid."

Veris nodded, her mind beginning to race even though she hauled back on its reins with all her might; fear trickled through her, thin and acrid, like some light poisonous liquid lurking atop clear water. Everyone in the village, everyone in the valley, even those several days' ride from the north woods, knew not to go into them.

But no one had told the Tyrant that, and so perhaps no one had told his children. Or, worse yet (much worse), someone *had,* and their curiosity had impelled them to go adventuring.

It really was only children that the north woods captured anymore. And even then, it was not the woods themselves but what lay within them. The south woods were used, and had been for many generations: carefully stewarded in terms of harvesting and planting trees, seeding berry bushes and planting tubers, cutting trails, keeping them signed and marked, hunting the game within, clearing debris from the streams.

The south woods were tame. The others, the north, were wild. You could not go in further than where you lost the light—five or six trees, usually, they were so old and thick. In that thin strip you might pick herbs, gather twigs, or hunt squirrels or hares. But you could not go in deeper.

Never, never, never. It had been drilled into them their entire lives; they had taken in the fear of the place with their mothers' milk. One more step and you risked falling into the Elmever. Where the other people of the woods lived. And they would not give you up.

And the Tyrant had found that out, hadn't he? When he had come. He had sent a detachment into the north woods, and they had not come back . . .

With her terror-sharpened eyes Veris spotted, she was certain, the children's mother next to the throne, not daring to lay a hand on it. Shockingly young, she seemed half Veris's age, but that could not be right if the children were as old as she thought they were. But fear had a way of changing your face too. The woman looked barely adolescent, thin, flat-chested, her fawn-colored hair intricately braided and studded with gems, but her face haggard, dark-circled. Her plum-hued silk gown had slid off her shoulders in a way that should have seemed alluring, but only rendered her unkempt now, and made her collarbones look pitiful rather than seductive. She would not speak, Veris thought, to cry out for help. From Veris, from her husband, from anyone.

"What do they look like?" Veris finally said. "How old are they? What are their names?"

The Tyrant grunted, and servants staggered over under the weight of an immense gilt frame containing an oil portrait nearly as tall as Veris herself, showing two children and a brown-and-white hunting hound sitting alertly at their feet. "This is not recent," he said, pointing. "But they are much the same. Eleonor, the girl. Is nine. My heir. Aram, the boy. Is seven."

Veris studied the painting, her mouth dry. The children were larger than life, and the artist had been talented, perhaps dragged in from abroad, as the Tyrant sometimes did. He was said to be a man without culture but with vanity, and that could be a dangerous combination for the artisans he conquered.

The children looked very much like one another, Veris thought, or the painter had made them so; they looked ineradicably like siblings, and like siblings who had picked up all each other's facial expressions and mannerisms so that they resembled each other even more than they naturally would. They wore similar velvet suits of burgundy and navy, trimmed with gold braid. Very white skin, like his, and the same black hair, and large brown eyes from their mother.

"Might the dog be with them?" Veris said, not hoping for much.

"No. We found her chained in her usual place. The children do not have the key."

Veris nodded. Oh spirits, oh lights, they were so young. *Poor things,* she thought, and almost slapped herself for it. Yes, poor things, out there without their good dog, poor children of the monster before her. And yet . . . Veris knew she was being unfair. They were innocent of their father's evil. The old women of the village would say they were tainted with it, but there was no taint in blood alone, truly. Veris knew that well enough from experience.

"I thought at first," the Tyrant finally said, his voice thickening, "bandits in the woods. Or some enemy of my reign . . ."

Veris shook her head slowly. "My Lord, I assure you

there are no . . . bandits, no brigands, living in those woods."

"But the nurse tells me people live there. Many people."

"It is complicated . . ." Veris's voice trailed off. The nurse would have tried to explain this as well, and been unable to. How could she do any better? And she was acutely aware, too, of something else that the Tyrant might or might not know by now: that she had but a single day to get the children back, if she was going to get them at all. And that day was burning away in the strong golden light of morning.

"The north woods themselves are . . . are probably perfectly safe. Like the south woods. But inside them, they are . . . *another* woods. Not the same. And when you are inside you cannot tell the difference between the north woods and this other place . . ."

She glanced away from the Tyrant's frozen face just in time to catch the expressions of the two guards on either side of the throne. Local boys, she thought. See how they look: terrified but also knowing. *They* had known better than to go into the woods as children.

In general, if you knew that your child had gone into the woods, you simply held a funeral: they were gone, they would never come back. But no one had told him that. All they had told him was that she had once succeeded in this impossible thing. *And the more curst I for it,* she thought.

"Get them," the Tyrant said. "I have given you all I know. And in secret. Say nothing, lest someone else creep in there and seek them out for their own gain. Do I make myself clear."

"Yes, my Lord." She tried to rise, and found that she could not; she was shaking again, though the room was quite warm now, and her legs had gone dead. The guard strode over and pulled her up, fitting his gauntlet somehow right into the bruises that already bloomed on her arm, so that she snarled with pain, her eyes watering.

"We . . . we have a day," she said quickly, breathlessly, before she could be dragged out. "That is all the woods give us. But I must return to the village, I must prepare for the journey . . ."

"Very well. Take her back there," the Tyrant said, waving at the guard.

And then she made her first great mistake: she added, "And in exchange, my vill—"

"In *exchange*?" He moved faster than she had ever thought possible, like a slung stone, making her cry out and try to dodge even as the guard held her fast. He crossed the space between them without sound, as if his boots had not even touched the ground, and seized her by the throat with one icy, powerful hand. "In exchange?

You dare, you worm, filth, you ask anything of *me*? If you do not recover my children your village will be razed to the ground and *burnt,* and we will roast your people alive upon it and *eat them.*"

Veris panted, unable to reply; the arched ceiling in her view, still crisscrossed with the old chains for hanging victims, began to fade to black. The Tyrant thrust her away with a snarl, spat at her feet, a wine-stained spatter like blood, and turned to the guard. "Take her back. Let her 'prepare.' Leave your two most *cinacth* men with her family. If she is not back here in a day, kill them first, then destroy the village."

"Yes, my Lord." The guard hauled Veris back toward the great open doorway, its tapestries now snapping and cracking at them in the freshening wind. Veris did not know what word the Tyrant had used, for it had been in his own tongue, which most people here still did not know; but she could guess, and she wept, a little, as the guard bundled her back into the carriage.

~

Her aunt seemed surprised that Veris had returned, but said only, "Will they be coming in for tea?"

"No," Veris said, glancing back at the handful of guards waiting silently in the front garden. A few had also crept to the back, she knew, to guard the door in case she still, unthinkably, tried to escape.

Veris shut the door slowly on them, to indicate courtesy, and leaned on it, trembling, eyes shut. Big, calming breaths, she thought, that's the ticket: but her chest would neither fully rise nor fall.

"You'll faint in a minute if you keep that up," her aunt said. "Come to the kitchen."

Her grandfather put the kettle on, and sat; and Veris sat too, and put her head in her hands while her aunt moved quietly behind her.

"I don't have long," Veris said through her fingers. "In fifteen or twenty minutes they'll come in here and pull me back out."

"What for?" said her aunt.

Veris shook her head.

The noises paused for a moment; resumed, more thoughtfully. Veris pictured it all in her head: sawing off slices from the loaf of black bread, buttering it, putting three eggs into the pan, crushing herbs. One, two, three eggs for luck; one, two, three herbs for luck. She sniffed lemon verbena, grassthyme, black mint. "I can't eat all that," she said.

"You'd better," said her aunt. She put her hand on Veris's head for a moment, then turned back to the kettle. "You haven't got long, you said."

How could she consider escape? It was unthinkable; she must keep these two safe if she could, having failed to save the rest of her family. For her parents had died a year into the war of conquest, before the Tyrant's full forces had even arrived in their valley. (*Don't forget that, don't ever forget. Mother first. Then Father.*) And her father's father had taken her in, little starveling thing as she was, twelve years old, and him stooped and old, for she had been such a late baby; and a few years later, in the thick of the fighting, he had also taken in her aunt, who was not even blood but who Veris had always loved. Widowed now, and all her children, Veris's cousins, dead.

And the three of them had lived here after the armies arrived and the fighters of the valley had simply set down their weapons (not out of cowardice, but because their valley had been conquered so many times—again and again and again, when you went back through the years, and there always came a point when you knew for sure that fighting would do you no more good).

In this case they had voluntarily disarmed, and in some haste, not only because the few remaining fighters had been outnumbered (and consisted mostly of elders and teenagers who could swing a sword), but because the Tyrant's rule always began with retaliatory pacification. All across his still-growing empire were places bereft of their original inhabitants, where he had decided that since they had vexed him in their resistance, he would ensure that they would never fight again.

Sometimes this was like blunting the horns of a troublesome bull, and he would confiscate their weapons and sink their ships. And sometimes it was slaughter: he simply killed everyone there, and resettled the area with his own veterans and bureaucrats and their families. You did not know which was which until the steel-shod and steel-wheeled army showed up at your door.

Veris roused herself, thinking of this, and patted her grandfather's shoulder, and went upstairs to prepare for the worst day (perhaps second worst; she did not know yet) of her life. In her room she washed up and cleaned her teeth and put her hair in a tight braid, then wound the braid into a bun and fastened that into place. In the Elmever you always had something seeming to confuse your eyes; that would certainly not be her own hair.

She had good britches now, which she had saved up to buy from the fair instead of making them herself (she could sew simple dresses and shapeless robes, but little else, and her aunt could not teach her). You might have to run in there; britches were better than skirts through the dense undergrowth. Thick woolen stockings, treaded boots, chemise, woolen sweater, leather vest.

Into one vest pocket she placed such tokens, wrapped in a handkerchief to keep them together, as she had used the first (*only, it should have been only*) time she had plunged into the woods: not powerful as such things went, she presumed, never having met anyone else who Knew Things the way she often did, but powerful to her because of memory, of love, and of hope. For wayfinding they might be useful, but to keep her firmly planted in the world of the living was more useful yet.

A small but perfect cube of hard smithy's coal she had found one day near the river; a chestnut that had fallen into her dress pocket as she had visited her parents' graves; a tiny wooden boar her father had carved, rubbed smooth from file and rasp and her years of constant handling.

What else? She paused, rubbing her forehead, then roamed the rest of the house. Things for a journey that might be brief and might last forever. Canteen, lantern, candles, matches, grease pencils, knife, flint, twine, extra stockings. She stuffed her leather satchel and buckled it across her body so that it sat in the small of her back.

Hopeless, really. Still Veris wolfed her breakfast and accepted the bag of food that her aunt gave her, and took out the apples, marking each with her initials. Her aunt said nothing, her face calm under her thin halo of silvery hair. Her grandfather watched with grave alarm. *Yes,* she wanted to say to him, *now you know. Now you know exactly where I am going.*

She did not say it. She kissed them goodbye, apologized for the guards, tied her food bag onto her satchel, turned down her grandfather's silent offer of his old but very sharp dagger (unwise to shed blood, even a drop, of anything that lived in those woods), and opened the front door just as the guard was coming up the steps to get her.

"I am ready," she said.

He pointed at the carriage, then looked over her head. "You two," he said, gesturing at his guards. "Stay in the house. You two stay in the yard."

Veris swallowed, hard. Beg them for clemency if she did not return? No, there was no use. Even though two of them looked like locals, maybe even knew her family, everyone around here did in some way, they were not arranged in neat spiderweb strings like the families in the big city, but tangled together close like wool, with roots that ran into each other's histories like the trees in the forest. Maybe the guards would extend mercy on their own. It was the best she could hope for.

She climbed into the carriage.

~

It was early enough that the woods were perceptibly chillier than the rest of the valley; Veris crossed her arms across her chest for warmth as the carriage vanished into the distance. It felt as if she had stepped unexpectedly into a cold, deep pond. The air was sweet and damp with fallen leaves, nothing but trees, moss, mulch, no hint of the village's perpetual pall of smoke.

With unfeeling hands, she tightened the buckles of her satchel, unbuttoned a pocket to get her handkerchief and its tiny magics, unlaced and re-laced her boots. Then she took an enormous breath—her first really deep one of the day—and said quietly, "I have returned. I am one known to you. Please allow me safe passage to bring back those who are lost."

The woods said nothing. She hadn't expected them to and if they had she was fairly sure she would have screamed; if anything, it went still, the breeze that swept the canopy pausing for a moment as if listening, the hiss of the grass in which she stood falling silent. At any rate no matter what you said, those inside the Elmever would make their own decisions and play their own games, and nothing would sway them from their ways. Certainly nothing human. It had been more to comfort herself than anything else.

When she could put it off no longer, she stepped carefully into the woods, not looking back.

The carriage had, at her request, dropped her at the closest point of the north woods to the castle walls, where the Tyrant had said the dogs had scented the trail. And indeed, her first few steps showed her the oval droplets of scarlet spattered on the leaves and grass where the handlers must have whipped their terrified dogs half to death before vanishing from the other end of the lead, freeing the animals to run up the slope to the gray stone walls they knew.

This was not where the children's bedchamber was, but they could have easily walked around the walls in the dark and simply gone out the gate. Two small creeping forms in a dark, silent night, nothing big or armed or threatening; the guards had probably not even noticed.

Oh, what had they been thinking? Veris walked slowly despite the urgency that already burned in her chest, studying the vegetation underfoot. Well. If you didn't know any better. It was just . . . well.

The temptation of it all: herbs still growing at this time of year, so tender they would be bruised by a child's bare foot; friendly shrubbery, perfect for hide-and-seek; rabbits to practice archery on; fat blackberries, plump hazelnuts; the great black- and gray- and violet-barked trees rising into unseen heights, a canopy so far up you almost could not perceive individual leaves, only their shouts of crimson, amber, gold, and the feathery dark streaks of the evergreens thrust out into them like ink. Squirrels darted from branch to branch, both the gray and the red.

And there would be other things too as she went along; her memory supplied her, unhelpfully, with images of snouts drooling and panting in the darkness, of fangs and claws, things that moved in silence even on these loud, dry leaves.

But it was beautiful in a way the south woods were not beautiful; it held this quality of age, weight, of mass and depth like a mountain. Maybe the roots of the trees went down as far as their branches went up. Someone here probably Knew.

In fact: she took the handkerchief from her pocket and rubbed the chestnut with her thumb. Nothing changed; no Knowledge settled upon her in a golden mist; her hearing remained the same, perceiving mostly the sound of the cool breeze through the trees, a constant soft murmur like the sea. It was a lovely morning, and that made everything much worse somehow.

Veris put the handkerchief away and looked around till she spotted a bird, a plain brown stone-wren, frozen on a branch a handful of paces away, hoping in the way small birds do that it would not be noticed. "Hello," said Veris. "I won't hurt you."

The bird twitched, flickered up the branch, returned, fixed Veris with one glass-dark eye. "Hello," it eventually said, then vanished into the safety of the leaves above.

Well. That was something. Birds did not always have

useful information, but to speak to them at all meant that at least some of her previous ordeal in the woods had been useful; she had not gained the ability until the last few minutes of that day, and so she had expected it to vanish as soon as she re-emerged into the real world.

Slightly cheered, Veris kept walking, continuing to scan the shrubs and bushes, the grass and the low-hanging leaves, for any clue of where the children might have passed. It was too much for her wood-skills, she knew, to find anything like a single hair caught on a branch, or a scrap of their sleeping-clothes, but it was surprising how often you could spot a footprint on a mat of bright leaves, or in the wide patches of earth damp from the night's dew and mist.

She called their names quietly, leaning down sometimes in case they had managed to stay close to the edge of the woods and taken refuge in a hollow or stump to wait for daylight. *Poor things,* she thought again, and was less irritated this time. It had been cold last night, a proper apple-frost (though of course you needed more than one for good fruit), and Veris had been grateful for the thick blankets and the well-sealed seams of her attic.

And the children must have been even warmer in their chamber; they probably had furs, even a fire in their room, which she tried not to resent them for. The castle was good stone, quarried three valleys away; it had taken five years and who knew how many lives for it to be built at the Tyrant's demand. In the distance the village had watched it rise slow and inexorable as a flood, seeming to speak sometimes, in the faint distant ring of metal against stone, the creak and groan of cranes: *I am here. I have taken over. I am not leaving.*

But the children *had* left. This was precisely the age when they'd be lost, she had to admit, the age when adventure held more allure than obedience or even fear, and when common sense had not yet developed. The child she had brought out the first time, for what little good it had done, had been eight years old.

Veris tried to imagine the escape, and sighed. Those two white-faced serious children with their black, black hair, as like as peas in a pod, each one another's only friend in the castle. The little boy whispering, half-laughing: *And if anything happens, it's all right, I'll protect you,* and the girl, bigger than him, older, giggling, *Of course you will,* because Veris's older cousins had humored her that way all the time.

(Till they died; till the father of these children killed them. So don't forget that either.)

Veris pulled her mind away from the past and tried to place it firmly on the now, and what might be. Had the children taken weapons? You never knew with the upper classes, with whom Veris admittedly had had little contact; but the few incidents of lords and ladies coming to carouse, or local nobles visiting the castle and pausing in the village, had suggested that they were armed to the teeth at all times. Sensibly, she suspected. If you had nothing, no one would kill you for it, but if you had *everything . . .* at any rate, out of a sense of hospitality or decency, out of fear of the Tyrant certainly, nothing had ever happened in these cross-class meetings. They came, they hunted or hawked (in the south woods only), fished in the river, stole horses, drank the two taverns dry, groped or honeytalked some local girls, and galloped back out again.

The further in she went, the thicker and stranger the light became as it filtered through the leaves; after half an hour it was like syrup where it fell on her hands and the pale sleeve of her sweater, or like the orange sun after a forest fire. She had seen no sign of the children, no footprint and no marking on bark or stone, and her path meandered and crisscrossed itself, and it was terrible that the woods were so large and there was no path.

Really, the problem was that people believed that there was some kind of . . . door, or gate, or at any rate some visible *thing* that let you enter the Elmever, and it was thought that this lured children in some way, tempted them with sparkle or song to step through it.

The truth was much more dangerous, Veris knew. For

the world of those others was not at all through a doorway that alerted you to its presence, but was instead adjacent to the real one in a way that could not be perceived by human senses, and that was precisely why people went missing into it. At some point, you took a step, and you were simply *there,* and you would not see the difference between it and the true woods, and you would never take another step that led you back home.

Unless, of course, you Knew what Veris did; and even then, she reflected bitterly, that had been mostly luck, which had failed her in the end. She took out the handkerchief again and held the three tokens in her palm, touching each other. In legend, supposedly, there had been someone who had gone in and out with both accuracy and alacrity using cards—the colorful ones you saw sometimes at the fair, never for sale, the beloved tools of the fortunetellers. But Veris had not learned the cards, and she would have to make do.

"Am I near?" she whispered.

They did not speak either, but they were not supposed to; the cube of coal warmed slightly in her hand though, and she nodded and turned that way a little and walked and asked again. After ten or twelve of these forays she added, "To the children, I mean. Not to the . . . place. In general."

A faint, golden haze appeared above the three objects

for just a moment, as if a sprinkle of sand had blown away in a breeze. If Veris had blinked, she knew she would not have seen it. They had to confer, it seemed; and her arm was getting tired, so she put them in her britches pocket and let them talk.

"Aram," she said to her hip. "That's the boy. And Eleonor, the girl. Isn't that such a pretty name? I wish I'd gotten that name."

The tokens said nothing. Veris spotted a flat-topped stone half-buried in the undergrowth and walked over to sit on it, dusting away a light coating of broken leaves and dirt with a bough carefully picked from the ground. The rules were vague but should not be broken: don't cut living wood; don't shed any animal's blood; trade if you must, but do not negotiate. And certainly never accept any "gifts."

"Veris is a name in the Tyrant's tongue too," she added, just for something to say. "Usually given to boys, though. I think he was a little surprised to see me. He must have been expecting some strapping adventurer."

Even as she said it, the woods around her rustled, and she leapt to her feet just in time to dance out of the path of a young boar moving at full gallop, in deathly silence, so close that just for a moment she smelled the acid of its running breath. It summited the stone, becoming airborne, a strange bird, then landed with a grunt, pivoted swiftly, and sprinted off to her right, into the greater darkness.

Barely thinking, Veris scrambled for the closest tree with branches that looked strong enough to hold her: a twisted elm, dead but sturdy, and close, like all the other trees here, to others. She clawed her way up, wincing as leaves and bark fell into her eyes, crawled sideways to another branch, and managed to get a few feet higher. And just in time: below her, not more than a few frantic heartbeats before she stopped moving, slunk a handful of sleek creatures.

Wolves, either broken off from their main pack or a tiny, hungry pack of their own, going for a youngster because they did not dare hunt a full-grown boar. The fur on their backs was clumpy and ragged, ruining the effect of their elegant movement through the brush. Veris tried to calm her breathing, to focus on the swirls of brown, gray, and white that she could see from above, their long mangy tails. Hungry. Yes.

Two of them darted immediately after the boar (Veris could still hear it crashing through the leaves, though distantly now). And two stayed, and stared up at her, their mouths hanging open, red lined with black as if they had been drinking ink. Were these already creatures from the other realm? Or were they ordinary wolves, and exempt from the rules? Well, it didn't matter; Veris had turned down her grandfather's dagger, and the little knife she had taken wouldn't even penetrate their fur.

"Shoo," she said quietly. "I'm not food. I'm *looking* for people."

One of them leapt to its hind legs, startling her, and scrabbled at the bark with its claws. Veris clung more tightly to her branch, and pressed her cheek to the tree, feeling her blood thump against it, quick and panicked. No, it was all right, it was all right. It had just given her a start. They couldn't climb up here. They were *dogs*.

Dogs that would, she suspected, circle back around once she left the tree and take her down. Fresh prey. "What are you?" she whispered. "Only, I feel that it's relevant to my future plans."

She wasn't as high as she had originally thought, she realized. Only five or six feet separated her from the wolf's clawing paws. "Which one are you?" she said again, then exhaled slowly in relief as the final wolf growled to the one that was clawing her tree, and they both loped off after the others. *Yes, begone, go get some fresh pork. Leave me be.*

But they might be back if they didn't, because she was tasty too, and larger than a squirrel or rabbit, and less lethal than a boar or a deer. She dropped down rather than climbing, wiped her face with her sleeve, and walked as fast as she could without running what she hoped was deeper into the woods, trying to keep her back to the castle walls, which she had long stopped being able to see.

And that was another option, too, wasn't it? Things lived in this forest that did not live in the south woods, the good, tame, hunted-out woods, large though they were. Wolf and bear, lynx and elk, wolverine, who knew what else. Things that were not even supposed to live in the woods lived in the woods here. Things you only saw in other countries or on plains or mountains lived here. If a tiger had leapt out at her she would not have found herself very surprised in the moments before her death.

She got out the tokens again and placed her back against a tree, glancing around worriedly in the thick amber light, shadowless and therefore bereft of directions. "Come on," she whispered. "Come on, come on."

There: the most minute movement of the boar statue on her palm. She pocketed them again, quickly, and half-ran that way. It was bad to run; things would chase you. Still, she could do no more than slow to a clumsy trot, which already felt worse on her feet and knees than either running or walking. The first time, she had been younger and braver; *Yes,* she thought, *but now I am wiser, I hope, and never mind my back. If I survive this, I'll spend a week in a hot bath.*

But the trees seemed to squeeze themselves closer

together as she walked, so that she had to detour around first single trunks, then clumps of them, then walls of them; and the occasional stones that protruded through the thin soil seemed to shuffle and grow, so that on turning her head suddenly she might realize that one had come up beside her, apparently without moving, and plugged a clear pathway through the forest.

Patience, patience. It had done this last time too, and even though you could not technically be lost in a place without roads or directions, still she had lost her way several times, and burned away too much of her day straightening out. Patience: the tokens were not powerful, and neither was she, and so they would have to move slowly, and in spirals, as the forest desired her to do.

At the very least, she thought, tugging her boot out of a fist made of roots that had formed around it, this was proof that she had indeed, all unsuspecting, strayed into the Elmever. No fanfare, no thunder, no shower of magical light. She had taken a step, somewhere, and here she was.

Was the air different in here? She paused, sniffed: yes, maybe a little. It was colder too, but that might have been the loss of the light, for the gold of the day grew ever darker as she went on. There were no more squirrels; there were birds though, indistinct all around her, small and quick. She called out to a few, asking if they had seen human children, but they all said they could not say.

"That's like a yes," she said, pausing to catch her breath and drink some water; a crow who had deigned to answer her cocked his head, far up in his pine tree and therefore nearly invisible in the branches except for the gloss of his feathers.

"It isn't," he said.

"Yes it is, a bit. If you had said 'No, we haven't seen them,' that would be a no. But 'We can't tell you' sounds an awful lot like a yes." She screwed the top back onto her canteen and stowed it away; his eyes followed the glinting thing eagerly.

He said, "Have the others been saying 'Can't tell you'?"

"Yes, they have."

He considered this for a moment, and seemed about to speak again, then leapt heavily off the branch and flew away. Veris swore under her breath and got up. Something big was snapping and shuffling through the undergrowth behind her, and although that was the direction the tokens wanted her to go, the forest did not. She would have to go around, and be canny about it.

It was hard to tell how long she spiraled and circled, how many trees she had to climb and drop down on their far side to get through, how many eyes peered at her from the undergrowth or worse, much worse, from far above her. But the day was burning away, she knew that much.

She mustn't let it make her panic, or she'd just lose her nerve and run screaming through the woods, howling for the children, drawing the attention of things that no doubt already knew she was here and were allowing her to live on their sufferance or curiosity for now. If you were quiet, if you were quick, you might make it in or out. Panic was the enemy.

Wasps hummed brightly around her, seeming half-made somehow, like scraps, broken pieces of the dimming yellow light. After the apples in her bag no doubt. And whatever else her aunt had thrown in there. That paused Veris for a second, and calmed her, as if she had been treading water but her toes had suddenly found something flat and firm in the abyss.

Aunty Daria. Seventy-something. Alive and well at the house. Think of that. A whole, real and true person, not like these little garbage insects. Worried of course but not in a tizzy. At her age you were past tizzies. Cleaning the house, glaring at the guards and pointedly ignoring any comments they addressed to her. Making tea for Grandpa.

Grandpa. Old Man Vorchus. Who in his youth they had called Stony, because he had shifted the rock that had blocked the canal to the river. By himself (with, he admitted to her later, a couple of levers people had not been able to see in the thick silty water). Who counted himself lucky to still see and hear at his age, nearly a hundred, and to still garden, and raise his rabbits. Alive and well at the house. Alive and well. Their neat, blue-painted house with its red front door. Red for luck. They both believed in luck.

"I will go back, and I will see my people," Veris said softly to the woods. "And you will not stop me."

Stay calm. Walk on. She waved the wasps from her face, uncaring of the ones that followed at her back, and kept moving, only occasionally pausing to consult the tokens now; they were moving only minutely, as if they were tired, or afraid of being spotted by something, and she couldn't blame them. The birds watched her closely when she asked them questions, but had stopped replying as well.

She climbed what looked for all the world like a masonry staircase, three tall blue stone blocks slick with moss and greenish water, and at the top peered down a long corridor, bordered on either side with bowing willows and weedy birch. Her pocket felt warm, but she did not need to take out the handkerchief to see what message was being sent. Very well: into the maw of the thing.

It wasn't so bad at first, except that there seemed to be no end to it, and the light faded entirely; she paused to spark her lantern, which was one of the collapsible miner's types and metal instead of glass. Keeping the light low, she shone it mostly down near her boots, to see whether she was about to step into or onto something that might break an ankle. But the path went on, smooth dirt carpeted in dead leaves, and there was no sound except the shuffle of her steps, which she could not avoid.

"Eleonor?" she whispered. "Aram?" Nothing. That was all right too; no reason for them to stay in here, in the dark.

The old women of the village sometimes swore that there were rhymes you could say if you strayed into the Elmever, or prayers to the old gods wiped away several invaders ago; or talismans, not like Veris's own tokens but stamped pieces of tin or lead that you could keep on you to get home; or a dance you could do; or herbs to rub on your boots; or shapes you could build out of fallen twigs that had some kind of protective and relocative power. None of them were true, but Veris felt the tug of fear inside her that made her wish they were, and so she understood why the old sayings kept coming around. It would have been good, so good, if there was something, anything she could do, to change a whit of this.

Something moved in the corner of her eye and she froze, simply stopped moving, hearing nothing but the faint hiss of the trapped candle in her lantern and the leaves moving overhead. No, something else too . . . not natural. Almost like a sheet on a clothesline, but . . . she inhaled to call for the children again, then swallowed it as something moved swiftly behind the line of trunks, large, softly glowing, twisting in midair like a feather.

Don't move. Do not *move.*

She had seen one of these the last time, not golden like this but pale blue, what difference did it make, some unexpectedly huge flat creature or spirit or something that she did not even have words for, flapping and writhing above the ground, feeding on a dead deer. And in silence, terrible silence. It hadn't spotted her, and had eventually flown, or blown, off, like a silk scarf caught in a breeze, trailing droplets of blood behind its unstained skin. If skin it was. She had tried not to think about it, had only seen it in her nightmares for weeks.

Veris moved one hand very slowly to meet the other, and closed off the aperture of her lantern, and waited in the dark. The thing drifted closer all the same, silent, spinning, yes like a scarf, she had not imagined that, it even had patterns on it, the way a snake had patterns, artful curves of leaves and vines. Like a made thing, but who would make such a thing?

Everything in her screamed at her to run; on her last journey she knew she would have. Now, she told herself to stay still, and she did.

But supposing the children . . .

No, don't think about the children. Think about the next

breath. Then the next. And don't move your head to follow the thing.

A high, thin scream split the air ahead of her, and the glowing thing whirled away toward it, and almost without meaning to so did she. That had not been an animal's scream, not anything that lived around here, not anything that lived in the woods or the Elmever itself, it was a human scream, but higher, thinner, and she pounded down the dark corridor of trees toward the dim light on its far side, knowing she could not outpace the flying things, running anyway.

And on the far side, of course, there was nothing, and when she turned the corridor was gone, was only the familiar tree-trunks and bushes and grasses and stone: because there was no other way for the trap to work. Distant laughter sounded around her, as far away and high as birdsong, but there were other noises, closer: the laughter of children, sobbing, another scream. This time she stopped herself after a few steps, and paused, resting her hands on her thighs, panting.

It was a trick, or some of it was a trick; that was the way here. Like the way the place sat against the woods, though, you would not know which of it was a trick and which was not; it was not as simple as black and white. Some of the noises were almost certainly memories, recorded somehow and replayed to taunt her now that the whole place knew she had come here with a purpose, and not by accident. Some of the noises were probably children that had come in here long ago, and perished. Some might be real, but not here. Some might be animals or peo ... well, creatures, doing imitations. Unless she caught them in the act she would never know.

And as for people: she had told the Tyrant that no one lived here. That was not strictly true. What did not live here was people, and even *that* was not strictly true, because nothing was. They were people-ish, and they had no name, and sometimes they did not look like people, even though they could speak. This place was their home, though, and whatever it took to keep it that way, they would not shirk to do it.

Veris breathed normally again, and meditatively got out her canteen, and drank a few sips, and put it away, and listened to the voices of the children around her. Examined, her tokens gave her nothing; perhaps she had finally asked too much of them. Part of her wanted to scream; part of her, somewhat hopelessly, suggested that she just think of it as giving them a little rest, not that they were dead. There were no birds now. The flapping thing must have frightened them off. And that was fine if they had been spying on her anyway, she thought, irritated. *Useless things.*

Still, it felt lonelier now, and the air held a new chill;

she rubbed her arms as she searched, and breathed on her fingers. Should have brought a coat, maybe gloves. The children would be even colder. *Well, if they had just stayed in their warm chamber in the damned castle* . . . no, there was the anger again, and that was worse than the fear. It wasn't the guards' fault, it wasn't the children's fault, it was nobody's fault. If you had to blame somebody you could blame the Tyrant for building here in the first place, but he was going to settle somewhere, and he hadn't known about the north woods. Or her own fault, if it came to that, for not letting that child die, for going into the forest to get her when no one else had ever come back . . .

The light grew stronger ahead of her, and she paused, mouth trembling around a laugh. Yes, she had seen something like this last time, and almost fallen for it, because it would have been so easy if you didn't have your wits about you: an invitingly petite apple tree miraculously sprouting in the woods, its leaves still deep green, hung with cluster after cluster of perfect fruit. She knew that if she picked one of the apples it would be crispy and sweet and as cold as if it had been set in the river, and she also knew that it was about as likely to kill her as to bind her in eternal servitude to someone who lived nearby, watching their trap with a patience that rivaled any garden spider.

"No," she said out loud, and for emphasis sat down on

the hospitably flat stone beside it, as clean and dry as the surface of a table. The lowest of the apples hung just in front of her face like a cut gem, twisting slightly in the breeze.

"It's the symmetry, you see," she said, getting out her own food. "*Real* fruit always looks a little funny, it's got bulges, bruises, wasp bites . . . I mean look at these things. They're like sculptures. And the color, *really*. Come on." Close up they were not quite a pure red, but a deep or-angey-pink, almost coral, shading from stem down to the blossom-end, which boasted a little kiss of yellow, as if they had been dipped in gold.

"It's a very good effort," she added. *And it would work on children,* she almost said, then bit it back, unexpected tears stinging her eyes. If a similar trap had been set somewhere, the children would absolutely have eaten the apples, and her rescue mission was for naught . . . well, that was enough of that. Anything could have happened to them here. Apples were no more likely than anything else when you thought about it.

She wiped her eyes with the back of her wrist and got out a piece of hard white sheep cheese, a slice of bread to fold around it, and her own apple, marked prominently with her initials. It was a Duckbill Gold, which was to say, sour enough to make her ears ring; but she ate it any-way, right down to the core, and spit the seeds onto the ground next to her stone.

This, as it turned out, was some kind of invitation: for the air shimmered, sending several of the beautiful false apples thumping to the ground, and with a brief blast of hot air something emerged from nowhere and stared frankly at her. "You again?" it said after a moment, nose twitching.

"Me again," Veris said cautiously.

"And remind me of your name?"

"I certainly shan't." Last time she had seen but not spoken to this creature—or something very like. Smaller than her, skinny, dark-haired, like a cross between a man and a hare and a deer, antlers bone-white out of a wood-brown body, wearing only a loose cloak of leaves woven into some kind of net. Now, closer, she looked down at his three-toed feet, which seemed real enough, and were stained with mud and bits of broken leaf. His eyes were large, liquid, and reminded her of nothing so much as the night sky: black from corner to corner, filled with innumerable little glints of light.

He edged closer to her. "Is that . . . cheese?"

"It is." She tore off a chunk and chewed contentedly, as if it were not the same bread and cheese she ate almost every day.

His lip twitched anxiously as he surveyed what was left. "Give us a bite."

"Oh no no," she said. "I was told never to feed those that live in the Elmever."

He sat back on his haunches in a way that looked superficially human, and looked up at the apple tree, still glowing and humming as if she would fall for it, and back down at Veris. If he had stopped moving, she thought, he would look like a wooden statue. Glass or maybe ceramic for eyes. She took another bite of her bread and cheese.

They weren't all dangerous, not necessarily, she knew. If you attacked them they would defend themselves, and if you crossed them they might lose their temper; the important thing was to keep an upper hand if you could. She did not think she could, though. Her desperation must be scribbled across her face like ink.

"You know our name," he said slowly. His voice was reedy—*woody*, really, but she hadn't wanted to think the word. Like a shepherd's flute. "And you went out, and you came back in. I say. I do say."

She smiled at him, not showing her teeth. He smiled uncertainly back, then scratched at his exposed ribs, making a noise like a struck comb.

"I'll tell you what," she said. "You can have the rest of this, if you like. I know you can't take it from my hands, and I know it's been touched by outside lips but perhaps you can hold your nose and eat where I've eaten. If—" She held up a finger, and he withdrew the hand he'd already begun to hold out. Her heart was pounding. "If you will take me to the two lost children. You and no other."

"Lost children? Oh, there are so many. Fewer now. Perhaps you all have eaten of the roots of wisdom . . ."

"You know who I mean," she said. "E—the two that *just* came in. This morning. A girl and a boy. They would have smelled of costly things," she added, watching his nose dance back and forth. "And maybe a little of dog."

His eyes darted to the bread and cheese again; but she suspected that if he were to give her any information it would be solely because she had presented her credentials to him, and not because of the temptation of something they might never see in here. Perhaps he had eaten it once, she thought grimly, carried by one of the children that had died in here, and had never forgotten it.

"I will take you as far as I can," he said, and reached out his hand again.

She nearly swallowed her tongue. "No. You will take me *to* them."

"I cannot go where they are!"

But he did know where they were, and that was something. He could not betray her if they both agreed on the conditions, but how far was *As far as I can*? She said, "When you take me as far as you can go, will I be able to see them unaided?"

"No. But you will see the place they are kept."

She couldn't waste any more time; they might be here all day arguing and picking apart each individual word in their promise. "Very well. Here."

He stuffed what remained of the bread and cheese into his mouth, chewing with a relish that verged on ecstasy, his eyes closing (the lids were green and veined as a leaf). "Thank you. That was an unlooked-for treat. Now come with me."

~

There were no paths, so she had to laboriously crawl and slide down the stones, and haul herself through trees, while her guide bounced and occasionally glided ahead of her, showing no signs of impatience. She began to see birds again, but said nothing to them; whatever you knew here might be used against you.

"Your hair was darker last time you were here," he said conversationally as she paused to let herself carefully down the far side of a broken shelf of thick-rooted soil.

"Yes, I suppose it was." She fell, landed in a sprawl, and got up, dusting herself off and checking her buttoned vest pocket for the tokens. Still there.

"But you smelled much unhappier," he went on. "So much unhappier. It came off you like the musk of a rutting—"

"Thank you, I think that will be enough commentary on my smell."

And she *had* been unhappy, anyway; and she had feared for her life, and for the life of the lost child, and she supposed it had been a long time till she had smelled happy again. If the people of the village could smell such things. No one had commented on it, anyway. Only gone to the funeral, out of politeness, and then gone home and run through every single ritual they could think of to cleanse their homes of bad luck and ill spirits.

Eventually, and much to her suspicion, the way grew easier—the trees were thinner and further apart, allowing them to walk along a not-too-overgrown path, and there even grew a hint of blue sky far above the riotously colored leaves. Veris paused and stared up at it, astonished, then down at the ground, where light, real light, ordinary light, dappled her boots. Already she had been long enough in the dimness of the woods that the moving spots seemed strange and shocking.

The little man gestured to her and lowered his voice. "Now, I cannot go any further. But you see ahead, do you? Tell me true."

"I see a clearing in the trees like a meadow," she said. "And I see . . ."

"A house," he said. "With four doors. Yes?"

"Yes, I see it. Well, I can only see one door." It was

far distant—the meadow seemed both very small and quite long, in a very gradual slope up to a summit that might only have been a few yards above where they now stood—but it was certainly a house. It resembled many of the houses of her own village, actually: white plaster with colorful shutters, and a dark roof made of thatch or slate.

Silence fell around them, thick and damp, and the ever-present breeze died by degrees, till every leaf that remained on every tree fell still. A few fluttered down nonetheless, bright as coins.

"They will be in there," he said, now so quiet that she stooped down to hear him. His breath smelled of sap. "There are guardians."

"Guardians? What kind of guardians? How many?"

"I do not know," he said. "I am not allowed in this place, I tell you. All I know is what I hear from the others. They will . . ." He hesitated, glanced at the grassy clearing, back at her. "They will hurt you if they find you. Just as they would me, just as they would many of us. So we all stay out here. But that is where the children go first. If they live, they will be in there."

"Dogs?" she said. "Wolves? Something else?"

"I do not know." He turned away, then turned back and said, "Make no sound. That is all I know. That may not be true; but may I be struck down if I tell you a knowing lie."

"Thank you," she said softly. He nodded to her, then pulled his cloak tightly around himself and vanished.

Struck down by what, she wondered idly as she methodically checked all her clothing for anything that might jingle or clink or squeak. Something bigger than him, or at any rate more powerful . . . or perhaps just with power over him and his kind, and over nothing else. You never knew. And did it not make sense that there was a hierarchy in the Elmever, just as there was in the real world? The Tyrant ruled over his empire, and he had governors, noble families, administrators, soldiers, and executioners to do his bidding. At every level, wherever you went, you could not escape his rule; and whoever did the actual striking, it would still in a sense be him who struck you down.

My family is in our house. They are alive and well. They are alive and well.

She stepped from the shadow of the trees into the sun-dappled meadow. The grass was thick and fine, like fur; she allowed herself a moment's daydream about the unbelievable, prize-winning sheep and cows she could raise on such stuff. And nothing in the way of noxious herbs or weeds—only the luxuriant green grass and sporadic winks of flowers still in bloom, pink, white, yellow, purple. Fat black bees like ink splotches patrolled the blossoms, occasionally emerging into the sunlight as if gasping for air before submerging again. Nothing seemed very terrifying, but that was an illusion. They seemed to pay her no mind. The bees weren't the guardians, were they?

No. She saw the first one a few minutes later, and nearly screamed out of sheer surprised terror before quickly and quietly clapping a hand over her mouth. But it did not notice her, and continued to clumsily crop at the grass.

Not eat it, she realized: it couldn't. The mouth moved out of habit, the teeth ground out of habit, but the dead deer would never eat again. It was a big stag, a sixteen-pointer, and had probably been magnificent once, but now it was a hideous impossibility: dead, very obviously dead, rotting, with loops of blackened, slimy hide dangling from its pocked skeleton. The skull was nearly bare, still roped all around with greasy-looking tendon, and the eyes were long gone—just sockets, in which a small reddish flame burned, like the match she had thought she saw flaring in the eyes of the Tyrant.

There were others, many others, lying in the grass. Not just deer but bear too, horrifying hulks of exposed muscle and gut; and yes, wolves, solitary now, no pack, oozing in their decay alone. And things she could not even identify, just tangles of bone and antler, as if in death they had lain down one night too close to one another and woken up unable to extricate their various parts. Some seemed to have a dozen legs; some none.

Her knees went weak; in her stomach the sour apple seemed to reawaken and churn with renewed life. There was no clear path through the ones she could see to the house. She would have to walk around them, and cautiously at that, not only not to make any noise but because she could not see the ones who lay in the long grass till she nearly stepped upon them.

All right. Stay focused. It was still better than the exhausting climb and struggle through the trees, wasn't it? This at least was flat, and there was light, and nothing screamed or mocked her here. And the grass would muffle her footsteps if she moved with care. It was all right. It would be all right.

Last time, there had been no meadow, no house. And Veris had never found out just what had happened, not in any detail. *I walked in my sleep,* the girl had said, *and when I woke, it was in Dr. Ervun's house with you . . .* So young a child, Veris had thought, was not able to dissemble; she truly did not remember her time in here, and that was a blessing. Still, she had woken with nightmares, screaming, for so long, until . . . no, don't think about it. What did they do with children in the house?

No, don't think about that either.

She concentrated on placing her feet, sweeping her gaze to either side in case she stepped on or kicked something small. Imagine that, a dead squirrel say. *Un*dead. Or a rabbit kit, or a . . . stop, stop. Too horrible. Veris prided herself, generally, on having only the minimum amount of imagination needed to get by; but today had revealed abilities she had no idea she possessed.

Her mouth was dry, but she didn't dare get her canteen. If her guide had said no sound, what he meant was no sound.

How much meadow remained? She stopped, shaded her eyes: no, she couldn't tell. It was still either "twenty paces" or "about a mile," which shouldn't have been possible, but who knew how distances worked in here. For all she knew she was a five-minute walk from the castle walls still, and had gotten turned around again and again in this place. But the house was still there; it was solid, real, it had not vanished. If it too were a trap it would wait till she was in it to be sprung. A slender thread of smoke rose from its chimney, in a (she hoped) false suggestion of friendliness or welcome; if it was not the wood of the Elmever, what were they burning in there?

She swallowed and forced herself to keep moving. There was a time, she thought, when her aunt had softly and unemphatically and even reluctantly suggested that Veris find herself a nice young man, or a nice young woman, and build a little cottage of their own; and this wasn't, Veris knew, to get her out of the house, because there really was plenty of room for four people, even more. It was because her aunt genuinely believed that a life was incomplete without marriage. And she had never questioned it. And she never did, even after Veris had emphatically insisted that she would never marry, never wanted to, and if she wanted a cottage of her own, she would jolly well buy the land and move them out herself . . .

Veris stopped, shocked at herself. Why was she thinking of that now? Oh, there was an enchantment over this place that the rest of the forest lacked, that was for sure. Where the rest of it was merely impatient and mischievous, this was evil. Things that she had considered long dead, and completely done with, were coming back to life, and just as with the dead guardians, it was a terrible and deliberate cruelty.

She could almost see it around her: magic not as words and spells but as poison, a faint smoky mist exhaled from the near-invisible flowers in the grass, from the tiny white mushrooms in the black dirt below her feet. What they breathed out was inattention, and inattention meant disaster.

Veris tugged up the neck of her sweater and put it over her mouth and nose. It probably couldn't hurt, she decided; and it might help. Just one step at a time, one step. Check foot placement first. Time was being lost but it was better than life. And the slowness was maddening, as in a dream where you are chased by something that should not be able to run but does, and outpaces you, and leaps upon you, but that too couldn't be helped. She gritted her teeth.

Somehow the house drew closer; now she could see the carvings on the closest door, not dissimilar to her own front door. Flowers, vines, feathers. The doorhandle was a smiling weasel, gleaming brassily in the shadow of the deep lintel. Its walls were white plaster, the windows thick and wavy; the roof was indeed thatch, though disquietingly dark. Most thatch bleached quickly in the sun, while this was black as the fur of a bear. And smoke still wisped from the chimney, she could smell it now. It did smell like woodsmoke. Just ordinary—

Her boot slid on something in the grass and in the split second before she hit the ground she realized she had been staring so fixedly at the house that she had stopped watching her footing, and it served her right, of course it did, the impact knocked the breath out of her and forced a squeak out of her mouth, *oh no, no, but it wasn't loud, it was very quiet, I barely heard it myself.*

But the guardians had heard it; and something reared out of the grass now, no more than an arm's length from her as she tried to get to her feet without making another sound, so close (she realized with a silent gasp) that if she did stretch out an arm she could brush her trembling, grass-stained fingertips across what remained of its snout. It had been a bear once, and what she had slipped on was some part of it: bowel or hide, something fatty that had filled the treads of her good boots and sent her flying. She stared up at it, at the flaring crimson light in its eyes, ringed with pink bone: like embers, as if their gaze could burn her.

Inside its rotting chest she watched every remaining string of tendon and muscle move as it drew back one clawed paw, and she ducked, trying to be silent again, and went to her hands and knees in the thick grass, and crawled quickly past it before rising again, glancing back to see if it would follow her, but it was staring ahead, still facing the way she had come, and if she had known what to pray to she would have whispered a prayer to it.

A moment later she realized how wrong she had been. For the other animals were rising, gathering, and there were more than she had first expected from seeing the handful from the lowest point of the meadow—dozens, perhaps a hundred. They rose dreamily as sleepwalkers, and some fell again, confused by their limbs, and did not rise. But the ones who were converging on her still came, and they came from all directions. Including, she realized with rising panic, from behind the house. If they surrounded her, she would never reach it.

It looked at first as if sheer luck might get her through (the three eggs at breakfast, the three pieces of bread, three herbs, yes, thank you Aunty)—for one of the things slipped and went down loudly, bone shattering like a crockery bowl being dropped down stone steps, and the others all turned on it. No loyalty in these guardians, it seemed; she found an open spot and darted through it. No, they were like any other guards, and only needed someone to fall for them to believe they could rise . . . she made it ten steps, twelve, before something slammed into her from behind.

This time her scream was sincere, and borne of both surprise and pain; she hit the grass hard enough to skid, though not far enough to escape a second blow from the same thing, this time high on her leg, flipping her over; even in her panic and terror she heard, faintly, the crunch as the lantern in her satchel was crushed by her weight.

The thing was a deer, or more than one deer, or . . . it was hard to tell, really, just a clutter of dangling legs held on by blackened strings of meat, and horribly, most horribly of all, threaded through the rib cage of one of them, a fawn—less rotted than the others and so far worse, bloated and streaked with blood still maroon, hopelessly tangled inside its captor and unable to get its skinny legs out. Veris gagged, partly with disgust and partly with the rising star of pain that began to bloom from her hip: and yes, one of the things had blood on its antler, fresh and new. Hers.

It reared back, lowered its head again, and she rolled away an instant before it could impale her, catching only the sleeve of her sweater and ripping it. The single scream had been enough: they were coming for her now in earnest, and leaving the one who had broken. In a moment it would be her who broke.

But she was close, so close; she had fought her way to within perhaps fifty paces of the house, and in one frantic motion she immediately knew she would regret, she kicked upwards at the thing's legs, sending it reeling back just far enough for her to scramble to her feet, reach up, and pull. Beyond her hope, one of the antlers (not the one with her blood on it, and she was oddly grateful for that) snapped off in her hand, spraying her face with chips of bone. As a weapon it wasn't much good, but it was better than nothing, and she swung it wildly around herself as she ran for the house again.

The guardians were erratic, unpredictable; they lunged for her and retreated, fell on their own, chased her with unbelievable speed, pushing the others out of the way, loomed over her, snapped at her legs as she ran. Nearly upon the doorstep she turned and swung the antler at the closest one, which she could not even identify, connecting with a shock that went all the way up her arm so that for a moment she thought she had broken her wrist, the same one she had broken as a child.

Instead the thing's skull broke off and went tumbling away like a round stone, and the body sagged to the grass, tripping the others, and she ran for the door, feeling the wind of their movement on the back of her exposed neck, expecting at any minute for something to tear through the fragile tube of her spine, but the latch gave, and she was in. She slammed the door behind her so hard that nearby something small fell off the wall and clattered onto the floor.

～

Veris had not been in a fight for a long time, and when she awakened from her faint she found herself shocked by the blood on the floor as well as by her instant, reflexive panic about the time. But she did not have a pocketwatch, virtually no one in the village did, and so all she could do as she wincingly cleaned and bound her shoulder and hip with torn strips of her chemise was fret about how much time had passed. Hours? Minutes?

The guardians were out there, and still, in her opinion, quite angry about her intrusion; through the thick wobbly glass of the window next to the door she watched them mill about in the grass, looking worse somehow in the bright unfiltered light of the meadow than they would have if she had encountered them in the woods proper. Even as she watched, something approached the glass and stared fixedly at her with a single burning eye, till she lost her nerve and backed away, staring around the room she had found herself in.

It was broadly spattered with her blood, and that couldn't be good; but aside from that there was something a little *off* about it, the way sometimes you looked at an apprentice carpenter's joinery and knew it wasn't exactly true. In the same way the whole house seemed to cry out for a shim to level it, a flat stone placed under something. The windows were wavy, which was normal enough, but so were the walls somehow, and so was the floor, so that the place where they met looked like the dark entrance of an animal's burrow instead of a corner. And it smelled piercingly of rot: animal, vegetable, fungus, leaf. Like a deer carcass not yet entirely picked over in the woods.

Veris moved carefully over the uneven floor, which looked like it was made from wooden planks but (she sensed) was not. It was all like that: imitating, with poor accuracy, a human house. Perhaps it had grown from the memories of the children who had come here, instead of first-hand knowledge or even a proper look ... and why had she thought *grown*? Well, it was of no account. The lapine creature of the woods had told her the children were here and he also claimed he could not lie; but they weren't in this room.

There was a staircase in the . . . no, *two* staircases. Even as she watched, her vision blurred and then refused to unblur, producing four: narrow, wooden-jambed entrances, two up and two down. Each step was carved with leaves, flowers, and small, mocking faces. Plump-cheeked and almost cherubic, they should have made her think of children too, but they did not.

She got out her tokens and glanced around again: and where, too, were the other three doors that the creature had spoken of? Up from here, she thought. Or down. What creature of the woods would know or care that doors are normally on the ground floor?

It was all the same to them. She must remember to think like the woods. Held flat on her sticky red palm, the boar would not turn, the chestnut would not tremble. The cube of coal managed a single, frightened twitch: the eye-dart of a prisoner on the bench, glancing swiftly at a co-conspirator in the galleries before dropping his gaze again to his lap. Distantly she heard laughter, voices, indistinct and in no tongue she knew.

Following the directions of her single speaking token, she stumbled through the house, up the stairs, down them again, along corridors that curved for too many paces to still be in the house; through a clumsy solarium filled with plants who laughed at her and tried to blow their pollen into her ears; through a library filled with blank books with viscid, thin covers.

These last arrested her in the house's labyrinth for a long time, too long, as she studied a volume picked at random from the tilting shelf. Her fingerprints remained on the cover of the deep-green book as she opened it, running her thumb along the edge of what they had passably mimicked as paper. It felt like the surface of a mushroom. One of the ones, she thought prudently, that you weren't supposed to eat. But grown whole and tome-shaped from the ridged bark of an oak or elm . . .

Veris put it back, and shuddered, and hoped mostly hopelessly that she had not made a mistake by giving the book her blood or her signature. Nothing in the Elmever was as it seemed; and many things were imitations of what they wished to be. And if she forgot that, she would never leave this place.

At last she felt a strange breeze upon her sweaty forehead—cold, damply scented with pine—and looked instinctively through the wobbly glass on the third or perhaps fifth floor, she was no longer sure. Outside the sun glimmered on the leaves of yellow and crimson; and every window was shut tight. Another place awaited her and she turned a corner, ignoring the stifled laughter at the level of her ankles, and found it.

The small, white-plastered house could not contain this lake, this lakeshore, this upturned bowl of darkness and stars, or the stiff young pine that grew alongside it like black feathers against the stars. She disregarded that too, and followed the smooth-pebbled shore.

There was no moon and she recalled that from last time—the creatures here loved only the stars; they did not trust the moon, which was too bright for them, and for the same reason they had even less regard for the sun. So the light here was thin and uncertain, and as she walked she cast no shadow.

On the beach, just a few paces from the lapping clear water of the lake, sat small cages made of fungus and bone, seemingly fragile (Veris knew they were not, were likely strong enough to hold a rabid bear). They were all empty, the doors sagging open, faintly luminescent. She gave them a wide berth, lest they snap at her, and went on; the stony beach was a strain on her wounded hip, and the fiery pain of the stab-wound itself was joined by a duller ache of taxed muscle. Blood began to run slowly from it and soak into her britches again, chilling at once in the constant, scented breeze.

But she was close; she knew she was close. And there: did two forms not huddle in the last cage on the beach, nearest the trees? She forced herself to keep walking, not to break into a run, and tried to keep her wits about her. No guards were visible but that did not mean they were not watching: to see what she would do, to capture her, worse.

She thought of her own house in the village, and the two elders within waiting for her to come home, and the two guards without, and the two guards within, and the dented, yellow-enameled kettle on the top of the iron stove. Alive and well, alive and well.

"And just whom might you be, hmm? Reinforcements? A change of guard for my tired old bones?"

Veris jumped, and regretted it; her hip ached and nearly collapsed under her. She turned slowly, favoring it, and looked up at the speaker who had just emerged from the trees and still brushed pine needles gently, fussily, from hair and cloak.

It was very tall, and in the darkness she could not see whether it held something in its hands or whether they were indeed long, curved claws; and she was glad for that, just as she felt suddenly, stomach-clenchingly glad she could not see its face either, only the eight small bright lights that shone in it. Its hair was long, silvery, and curled, and had captured not only pine needles small and gleaming like sewing needles but also a few cones, and acorns, and dead leaves.

"My sympathies for your bones," Veris said politely.

From the corner of her eye she saw the two small forms in the cage stir, sit up, clutch its bars. They did not speak and that was good; for who knew what they might say at this delicate moment to imperil themselves further?

Or what they had already said?

Veris took a deep breath. The guardian shuffled down the beach toward her, smooth round stones clattering under its feet. It wore a long ragged cloak that seemed like rotten hide, but Veris thought that would be quite unusual—they did not wear the skins of beasts here. Perhaps it too was fungus, or made of fungus, like the house. Gradually, moving only her thumb, she folded her handkerchief again around her three tokens, and placed it into the back pocket of her britches, wincing as the wet cloth stuck to her wound.

"Do we know you?" the guardian said softly. Like the creature Veris had shared her food with, its voice was strange—inhuman, but also not animal. Composed of lake-hiss, rock-click, tree-breath. Almost a song.

"No," Veris said.

"You have not been here before? Hmm? You can tell us. Go on."

"I have not been to this place," Veris said truthfully.

"It is where we bring visitors to our land," the thing added, still approaching. Veris locked her knees half-instinctively; if she retreated as the guardian advanced, she would be backed into the lake, and for reasons she could not even explain she fervently wished that not happen.

It kept coming though, speaking the time, till it and Veris were so close the wind almost could not pass between them.

"So that they may be examined. And questioned. Before they go to their new homes."

Veris blinked. All her life, she had believed that after the day was up, any child who had strayed into these woods was killed by its inhabitants; that they might be adopted out had not occurred to her. But it made no difference now; she could not allow either fate to befall these two. "I have come to take them back to their real home."

"What means *real*? The one we give them will be real enough." It paused, and flexed its claws, easily close enough now to swipe Veris's face off without straightening its arms. "And their happiness will feel real."

Veris shook her head. "Their happiness is not my concern," she said. "But I must return them to their home. Tell me how I can do so."

"There is no way. The cage is strong and I hold the key."

"There is a way," Veris said evenly. "For no creature of the Elmever would turn down a deal. Would you?"

The creature hissed, a small sound easily lost in the

wind through the pines. Veris stared into the darkness of the chest before her, where a living thing might have had a heart. Here it was only a cool darkness that rattled gently, like branches. "You would buy them from me?"

"I would consider it if I knew your price."

"Then I too will consider." It gestured at her, and they walked the few remaining steps to the cage, where Veris allowed herself a heart-pounding moment of relief and dropped to her knees, whimpering at the pain, to look inside.

"Who are you?" whispered one of them in a lightly accented treble; she could not see which. Only their dark hair was visible, shiny over their dark clothing.

Veris shook her head. "Your father sent me. Say not his name! Nor your own. Are we clear?"

Silence for several moments. Then: "Our what?"

Her stomach sank. So their names had already been taken from them—and for a moment she felt both anger and despair, for at the very least, no child from her village would have spoken their name. They did not all obey the instructions to avoid the north woods, but once inside, they would have known to obey all the rules they had been taught in the event of such foolishness.

Veris closed her eyes. No, there was no point to the anger, and she must not let it thicken her blood. They were innocent. And that bore remembering for other reasons: their father was the monster, his armies were the monsters. Not them. That they might grow up to have an empire of their own one day, that they too might be the murderer of millions, that was in the future; and it was a future that she could not forestall by leaving them here. They must all get out of the woods and take their chances on later massacres. Her name would not go down in history anyway, as the indirect causes of such things never did. Only theirs would.

Absently, she scooped up several stones, cold and round as snowballs, and put them into her satchel. One never knew when one might need a stone; and the ones in the woods were too root-bound and monolithic to give her any.

"Our new father is coming for us," said one of the children. "They said so. And soon."

"No, he cannot," Veris said. She raised her head and called out to the guardian: "Have you determined your price yet?"

"I think I have."

They met again, and closer to the lakeshore; Veris kept her eyes on the stones, mindful of the water, which was difficult to see.

"I would like," the guardian said, "two years of your life."

"Two years off the end, you say?"

"Yes. One per child. I think that is very reasonable. Or if you like, you could give me one year only; and choose one of them."

Veris pursed her lips, as if she were merely perturbed and her heart was not hammering nearly out of her chest. She was so close; and there was no other way to open the cage. Two years wasn't much, was it? If you were going to live to, say, eighty-eight, and might only live to eighty-six instead. The Thorns were a long-lived family. Look at Grandfather.

But supposing you went home with your *Two years wasn't much, was it* and died the next day, because you never did know when your time was up. "Is there no other price you will accept?" she said, trying not to wheedle or whine; how sensitive they were to such things here! "I could give you . . . a childhood memory, perhaps. My most perfect spring day . . . my first kiss . . ."

She tasted the mistake on her tongue bitter as wormwood even as she said it. *Oh no: never negotiate.*

"I want none of those things, and now the price is four years," the guardian said. "Two years per child. Or we will wait here, and you will see for yourself who has come to claim them as his own."

Veris liked the sound of that less than anything she'd heard in the past several hours. She swallowed hard.

Time was wasting. Time was wasting in general, she corrected herself, but also her own; and if she hesitated too long, the price might raise again. "Let them out so I can see them."

"So you can see?" The thing laughed, a small rattle of stones that seemed to foretell an avalanche, the sound so accurate that Veris flinched. "You think we are trying to fool you? That we have replaced them? I assure you, their new family would not stand for it; they are who they were when they trespassed upon this place."

"Well, nevertheless. I do not accuse you of deceit myself; I merely wish to see what I am buying."

Another rattling laugh. Veris trailed the guardian as it returned to the last cage on the beach and stooped over it; she heard the sound of no lock or key, but the children crawled out slowly and stood, small and uncertain, so that her heart ached with pity instead of leaping with triumph. And why should it leap? They must still return, and they could not return through the door she had come in. Too late she realized she should have added that to the initial deal: *And you must also sell me the way out.*

"Come here," Veris said to the children. They came obediently and she turned them this way and that by their birdlike shoulders, trying to see their faces in the starlight. Dark hair, yes; dark eyes, like the portraits. Like the woman she had thought might have been their mother in the throne room: her dark eyes had won the battle over the Tyrant's golden ones. And they did not smell of the woods, as she thought a made thing might; their clothing, thick and velvet, trimmed here and there with fur, was perfumed with the castle. Something rare and thick, like attar of roses. They looked up at her without hope, unable to see her face silhouetted against the night sky inside the house.

Veris turned back to the guardian; had she heard, somewhere in the forest, the crunch and thud of something big moving through the trees? Even if she had only imagined it, she could not spend more time here. Perhaps she could find their own way out, if the "new father" could be avoided. He would be angry that his prize had gotten away; a deal had probably already been made for them. That was the way it worked here. "I will take them," she said. "I will pay."

The guardian cooed mockingly, with an undercurrent of menace now that Veris pictured as bigger stones falling down the hill. Her hands glazed with sweat.

"So lightly do you hold your own life," it said. "Very well. Then the trade is complete. Take them and go."

Veris had felt nothing, but she knew in the way of Knowing Things that it had indeed been completed; and her own death had drawn four years closer. She would not petition the Tyrant to pay this cost for her even if she could, no more than she would invoice him for the rescue itself, the blood, the hours spent, the cost of the apples and bread and cheese in her pack, whatever else she had lost here.

They remained on the beach; the guardian watched them; the treetops were beginning to shiver and move, and a smell came to her of fresh resin, upturned soil. The house did not suddenly resemble a house again, and no doors appeared. Veris swore very quietly under her breath.

"Come on," she said. "Into the woods."

The children followed her silently as she gauged the direction the noises were coming from, and plunged into the pine woods perpendicular to it, moving quickly through the sparse young trunks, through a carpet of fallen needles that felt miles deep. The new father, if that's what it was, must be kept behind them; and so too the beach with its cages. When they were distant enough, Veris thought, she would take out her tokens again, and ask them for such guidance as they could give her. And she only allowed herself a moment, as they crouched and scurried through the darkness, for exultation: at least she had found them, and alive, and apparently themselves!

All we have to do now, she said, or even panted as they ran, *is get out.*

Behind them sounded howls: of rage, of pursuit, of righteous anger at the theft. Veris hoped her stockings and boots were absorbing the blood she could feel running down her leg; she felt faint, but fear spurred her on, and she kept the children on one side of her, so that they should not be separated, and after she felt she could not go on one more step, the noises faded, and they were alone, or so it seemed, in the starlit woods.

~

Veris would not allow a fire to be built, but she needed light, and badly; once lit, she had the taller child hold the lantern while she checked on her two antler wounds, which had stopped bleeding freely but still wept and oozed. Nothing for it but to sacrifice her spare stockings as bandages.

When that was done, they sat gingerly on the needles, protected behind the thickest tree they could find, and Veris examined the food in the children's satchels. "Did you get any of this from the forest?" she said, squinting at a handful of hazelnuts, setting aside packages wrapped in greased cloth. "Anything?"

"No," said the taller child. "We saved some of our dinner from last night."

"And we—" began the shorter child, and burst

unexpectedly into tears; they ended a minute later, and Veris handed over a clean handkerchief without comment.

"Wherever we go now," Veris said, "you must not eat anything you see. Nothing. Not one nut, not one berry, not one fruit. No matter how beautiful or safe it looks. Do you understand me?"

They nodded.

"Good. You can eat what you brought then." She gave it back, and turned up the lantern one notch; it had been crushed well and true when she had fallen on it, and the light it gave was half-smothered, smoky and uneven. Their meal was illuminated in flickers rather than a steady glow, so that she could see them for only a moment at a time.

"Oh," said the shorter child, chuckling, and looked at the apple Veris had given them from her own bag. "Vee Tee."

Veris watched impassively. "You can read?"

They both nodded.

"In our tongue as well as your father's?"

"Yes."

She got out a black grease pencil and turned over one of the cloths that had held their bread and meat from dinner. "This is me," she said, and wrote VERIS and showed it to them both.

"That's a boy's name," said the shorter child.

"It is not," Veris said crisply. "I am a woman, and it is my name, so it is a woman's name. And this ... which of you is the girl?"

The taller child raised her hand, and Veris repeated it with ELEONOR, then ARAM for the boy. Realization dawned on their faces, surprise and relief and something almost like shame as their names were restored to them. A name did not mean everything, Veris knew, but it didn't mean nothing either; and in here it meant more than it did in the world outside.

"The people who live here," Veris said, folding up the cloth and stowing it in her satchel, "cannot read the symbols of the outside world. Did you tell them your names when they asked you?"

Eleonor nodded, wiping her mouth on her velvet sleeve. "It's how it is in the court," she murmured. "They ask us our names and if we are our father's true children, and we always have to say."

Veris sighed. "It is your father who sent me," she said. "To get you out of here."

"They told us no one ever gets out," Aram said matter-of-factly.

"Well, I have gotten in and gotten out," Veris said. "And with a lost child alive and ..." She trailed off. *Alive and well*, she had almost said. But only one of those had turned out to be true. At any rate there was no sense detailing the child's fate to these two; they didn't know her and they never would. "So you will have to do everything I say, do you understand?"

Aram nodded; Eleonor cocked her head like a crow, and said, "How do we know you're not one of them? One of the . . . the people that lives in here."

"That's true," Aram said excitedly. "They can look like anything, they can look like anyone. We saw—"

"You will simply have to obey me," Veris said. "You do not have to trust me, if you wish. Your father sent me. I saw your portrait in the throne room. Your dog was still tied up in the courtyard; he did not tell me her name. Your nurse," she added severely, "has paid a terrible price for what you have done, and so have I."

The children fell silent; Veris tried to read their faces, as children's faces are transparent as no one else's are, and saw only that the words *your nurse* had perturbed them. Likely they loved her, inasmuch as children of royalty, she thought wearily, could be said to truly love any servant; likely they knew what Veris had meant by *terrible price.* Whatever distance their father kept or did not keep from them, tales of his deeds were their bedtime stories, and the great atrocities he had committed, and was capable of at any moment, were known to them.

"Why did you come in here?" Veris said. "And when?"

Eleonor hung her head. "It was my idea," she finally said. "When . . . I don't remember. They check on us about midnight. So after that. We share a bedchamber, you know, for now, but we won't next year, and anyway, our beds are quite far apart, with a window in between. We knew we couldn't get out the door because there are guards. So we went out the window."

"You . . . climbed down from the window. To come here."

"It's not so far a fall," Aram said eagerly, waving his hands to illustrate; Veris pulled the lantern closer to herself. "It looks like it is but it isn't really. You drop down onto the Wird Wall and then you can go around that because there's nobody and then there's stairs that go down to the Brocade Wall, and then you—"

"—have to get past the guards," Eleonor finished. "But they're looking out not in, of course, so then you can go down to the Var Wall, and then out through the gate."

"That's how," Veris said after a moment, "which I didn't ask. I asked why."

They shrugged, uneasy. After a while, Eleonor said, "It was just . . . beautiful, and . . . and it looked safe. And when Father takes us hunting we always go to the other woods. But they said he kept this one for hunting. And we wanted to look. I guess."

Veris sighed. "It doesn't matter. At any rate we must

be out of here soon. I don't know what time it is; and you don't know what time you left. But we only have a day before we must remain in here forever, before we are claimed as the forest's own. No matter how tricky we are," she added, before Aram could jump in, "and no matter what we do. Now do you promise to do as you're told?"

"Yes, we promise," said Eleonor.

"Both of you."

"I promise," said Aram. He looked up at her, and smiled, Veris thought, for the first time, impressed. "And I can fight, if we have to fight."

Veris smiled back. "Put up your blades, Aram. We eat nothing here; and we shed the blood of nothing here."

"But that's not fair. They shed *your* blood."

"Yes, because I was unlucky and foolish. We do not want any more of that. Now get up; I must ask for directions."

~

Veris asked the tokens how to return to the house, and they said nothing; perhaps, she worried, they were trying to communicate that they must return in a way other than how they had gotten in. But she didn't know how she had gotten in, nor the children, and the house was the only landmark she truly had. "Is there another way?" she whispered, focusing all her attention on them. "There has to be another way. Please, only show me how. We don't have much time."

She watched them rock back and forth only in time with her heart: cube, nut, boar. The children watched them with drowsy interest, the boy absently holding the girl's long velvet-covered arm with both hands. They would both be tall one day, Veris thought. Like their father: two big monsters.

"Are they magic?" whispered Aram. "Are you a witch?"

"A what?"

"Well, Father always said they have witches in the place he comes from," Aram said; he visibly wanted to touch the tokens on her palm, and held himself back with difficulty. "He said they're ladies that can do magic."

"No, I'm not one of those," Veris said. "It may be that I own some things that can do magic on their own; but me, no."

Aram nodded, disappointed. "I wish I could be a witch," he mumbled. "But I'm not going to be anything."

Eleonor elbowed him, impatient. "You are so," she said. "We *talked* about it. Don't you remember? I'm going to rule half of the lands, and you're going to rule the other half. At the same time. Because it's too much work for one person really."

"But Father said—"

"Never mind what Father said," she said. "I'm the heir and when I'm Tyrant, I'll do what I like, and I'll make you an heir too."

The chestnut, normally the least talkative of the three tokens, twitched sharply and rolled on Veris's palm so quickly she had to fumble and catch it with her other hand, slow and clumsy with her wound-stiffened shoulder. *Go,* the chestnut had seemed to say, or felt as if it said, putting invisible or nonexistent lips to the lines on her palm, *and quickly too.*

Veris stuffed everything into her vest pocket and patted herself down, then briskly frisked the children to make sure they would not drop or spill anything, feeling with envy that she could not deny the richness of their clothing, the softness of the fur. Too clearly did she remember shivering in her sleeping clothes in the throne room, as the cold autumn sun came in without warmth, like the eyes of the Tyrant. "This way," she said. "Quick and quiet as a mouse. I have reason to believe there is something after us."

~

She was right, too, and as they emerged through a kind of veil or even a light blanket of sweeping branches and twigs, into the ordinary dark amber light of the Elmever, the sense of pursuit and the sense of nightmare did not fade. It did not feel warmer here than the unlit beach; if anything, it felt colder.

But the light felt warmer, and that made everything feel unreal, and you could feel temperature in nightmares and dreams; Veris had been burned, frozen, frostbitten in dreams. She had woken weeping from nightmares of the hunt, in which something had chased her into a fire . . . it felt like that now, and the thing after them could not be seen, only heard. And, occasionally, smelled—a thick, predatory musk, which made Eleonor startle like a hare every now and then and bolt forward a few steps before she could stop herself.

Anything close enough to smell should have been close enough to attack them, and likely it was; and the terror of this fact strained them as if they had been running, all three. They could not outpace their pursuer and they did not dare turn and fight. They must make progress away from it and that was all.

Aram panted as he walked, trotting to keep up with Veris's long strides and one hand kept firmly in Eleonor's grip, his other on the blue glass gem of his dagger-hilt— as small as a toy, to Veris's eye, but still she hoped that her constant reminders would prevent him from drawing it when the thing eventually galloped out of the trees. For she knew what followed them, and she thought the girl did too; the boy, it seemed, less experienced at the hunt, did not recognize the smell as dangerous.

"I always thought they were," Eleonor said, glancing over her shoulder, "*nice*."

"No," Veris said. She glanced too, though she could not see anything but the tangle of woods behind them, and had not for some time now. "They're nice in paintings. And stories."

"And I thought they ate grass. Did you see one . . ." The girl hesitated. "Last time?"

"Yes."

"What are you *talking* about?" Aram squawked.

"Keep your voice down," Veris said. That the boy might panic had occurred to her; that he would try to do something recklessly courageous, as children do, seemed more likely, and if he darted away from his sister, he would head right toward their pursuer. Veris was in pain constantly now, and bleeding, and she could almost picture the odorous trail she was leaving: like a red silk ribbon fluttering in the constant breeze.

"You did this once before?" Eleonor said, tightening her grip on her brother's hand.

"Yes, just once." Veris hesitated; she was not a naturally prideful person, but her urge to emphasize how unwise the children had been was irresistible. "I'm the only person in all of history, as far as is known, to have gone into the north woods and survived. Myself, and the child I rescued. Everyone else, *everyone*, was never seen again."

They hurried on, glancing behind themselves often at the blameless woods. Eventually Eleonor said, "Did they pay you lots of money?"

"Who?"

"Whoever sent you in after that child. Last time. Or did they give you gifts? We usually get gifts instead of money. Jewelry and things."

"I didn't get anything."

"Then why did you go?"

"I think," Veris said, "we should stop talking now." *Monsters,* she thought clinically, speeding up as much as she dared on the uneven ground. *A monster who begat monsters, and I walk with them now; little tyrants. Well, I was not sent to mother them. I was sent to get them out alive.*

Imagine our land under their rule, though. Or just the girl: the heir. Imagine that. Did she have the careless transparency of a child, or was she a monster in the making? All around them the birds fell suddenly silent; she felt, or imagined she felt, or fear had heightened her senses so that she felt, the ground tremble under her boots, as if distant stones were falling from the mountains. Had the children sensed it? No, they walked on, their faces not more perturbed than before. Veris felt ill.

"Your mother," she said, keeping her voice low. "Do

you see her often? Does she stay in your chamber? Or nearby?"

"No," Eleonor said. "Father says since she's common, it's not right for her to teach us."

"Only him," piped up Aram, out of breath. "Because. He's the ruler. And we have to learn how to. Read and write like. Him. And maps. And fight and hunt."

"He takes you hunting?" Veris said. "Himself?"

"Oh, yes," Eleonor said. "Not often because he's usually away. Me more than Aram. We go to the south woods with bow and spear and just his personal guard, ten men. He has guns but he says those shouldn't be used for hunting."

Veris nodded; she had almost said *What are guns?* but in fact she had seen drawings of them a few times, and in person seen a small one, disassembled, during the war. Intricate as a clock, deadlier than any arrow, if it was to be believed. Something so dangerous it seemed like magic itself: a token like hers, but instead of being carved from wood or forged from metal, a shape pressed out of the poison some said you could make from century weed, so that a cube of it the size of her own piece of coal could kill ten thousand people or more. Imagine that: passing it from hand to hand and the hand falling away, falling to the ground, just from the touch. In such a fashion had guns been described to her. They would change the whole world, they said, once everyone had one.

She shook her head, keeping her face still, mind racing. Their pursuer was closing on them, and they could not race it across the roots and stone, could not plot a clear path through the trees. If it was possible to outwit the thing, that might be their only hope. Still moving, she climbed over a chest-high shelf of moss-slick stone, pulled Eleonor over, and together they reached back over to get Aram.

The light had absorbed all the shadows around them; they moved through a syrupy golden haze. Still, a shadow stretched across them now, crisp and black, crackling along the edges as if it were on fire, as if a flame itself had learned to cast a shadow.

And the beast cast it, and it was great and terrible, and its head rose to nearly the canopy of the forest, and the single horn scythed from its forehead curved and gleaming as a sword.

Veris nearly swallowed her tongue. For several seconds no one moved; then she tightened her numb hands on Aram's forearms, and lifted him over the stone to join her and Eleonor on the far side. All three could still see the beast, and it could see them.

The unicorn's eyes were blue and deep, and glittered like an ice-covered lake; its hide was white, with an unpleasant greenish undertone as if it were one of the soft white shelves of fungus that sprouted from the trees. "*You,*" it said.

Aram squeaked; the voice was terrible, low and loud, the roar of a beast, made worse by being perfectly intelligible. With some difficulty Veris compared this hulking warrior with the one she had seen last time: a slim thing, just bigger than an ordinary farmhorse, with a golden horn like a nobleman's rapier, a sword meant for playfights with friends. But they had been so close to the edge of the woods that Veris had simply picked up the child and fled into the winter sunlight, and when she had looked back, the beast had been gone.

This one would not be so easily evaded. Its legs were planted foursquare, haunches tightly coiled, as if ready to rear, or spring at them like a wolf; its hooves were as big as cartwheels. It smelled intensely of wolfish musk too, and feces, and blood, for all its apparent cleanliness. Like something torn-open already, splayed for the ravens and the rooks.

And its teeth were gray razors, and they glistened as it spoke. "You have my children," it said.

"They have been reassigned to my custody," Veris said. "I paid for them."

"Did you now. I paid for them first. What you have done you had no right to do."

"I suggest," said Veris, "you remonstrate with your associate near the lake. This disagreement has nothing to do with me."

It took a step forward, which by virtue of the length of its stride took it near enough to Veris that its shadow crossed over her, and the stone behind which she trembled and stood, and the dark heads of the children, staring with their mouths open.

"Come with me," it rumbled into its shadow. "I am your new father."

They said nothing; Veris, through the stifling blanket of her fear, felt a moment's gratitude. Better they say nothing than agree to something that the unicorn might present unexpectedly as a deal. It was how things worked in here, she thought, not for the first time.

She looked down at something small near her whitened, blood-smeared knuckles: a brown stag beetle, clambering over the mountainously uneven lichen that grew on the stone. From the corner of her eye, something else moved in the trees: something big.

Veris closed her eyes. Opened them. "When I say that you must do exactly as I say," she said quietly to the children, "will you do it?"

"Yes," they whispered.

"Exactly as I say. And when."

"Yes, yes."

"Good," she said. "Back away slowly."

"I would not do that if I were you," the unicorn said as they shuffled through the leaves, keeping their gaze fixed upon it. "Obey me! Me! *I* am your father, you belong to *me*! To the woods and to *me*!"

Veris's whole head rang with the thunderous shout; Aram whimpered and covered his ears. Eleonor was so pale that Veris worried for a moment that the girl might faint; could Veris run wounded, encumbered by even so slight a weight? Her everyday life had not prepared her for this now any more than it had all those years ago. But the girl stayed upright, breathing in little gasps through her mouth.

"Follow me when I say run," she whispered. "Turn. And run!"

Like deer they leapt, over the stones and the thick tangled roots, and they slid on mats of rotting leaves and fell to their knees and rose and spotted light through the trunks and ran for it and even when the light proved illusory and ever more trunks arrayed themselves ahead of their flight, they kept still the unicorn at their backs, and even gained something of a lead.

It didn't matter where they were going; Veris would have to find them a path later. If there was a later, if her plan, the work of five rapid heartbeats' worth of thought, worked. She did not think it would. "Make noise!" she said as she ran, breathless. "Shout! Clap your hands! Bark like dogs!"

And so for several moments they were a comical trio, like the one-man bands that sometimes came to the fair, this instrument strapped to this arm, that instrument strapped to that foot, everything connected, tears and sweat and spit rolling down his face as he played for their pennies—and yes, the stench of the unicorn followed after them, and a new smell on the breeze, of ozone, of something distant come inexplicably down to the ground, through the treetops, through the upper air.

Veris could not see it and she didn't like that at all, but it was their only chance, and she not only could not, but would not even if she could, shed a drop of the unicorn's thick and stinking blood.

She tasted her own blood in her throat and thought of death, hers and theirs; she thought of the village torched and smoldering under a night sky of ethereal beauty, and the bones of her family, and the bones of their house, giving off a small oily light. She thought of collapsing, and taking a nap. The unicorn might impale her before it ate her; you never knew your luck.

Instead, she shouted, "Silence! Absolute silence! You, dart off to the left when I say—and we will go to the right! Then freeze! Now!"

Eleonor shot off to the left like a startled rabbit, and Veris seized up Aram and lunged to the right, leaping over a gnarled mass of roots that seemed to raise itself to stop her, but it was too late, and she was over, and slamming her back to the tree, one hand clamped tight over the little boy's mouth, her other pinning his arms, holding him to her chest. All her weight was on her bad leg, but she did not dare shift now.

And the unicorn, which of course had been just steps behind them, very few of its steps, a few more of theirs, skidded to a stop where their scents diverged and screamed, turning his head to look directly at Veris, "Give them to me! Thief!"

But it was the only creature making a sound in the forest now, and the floating thing of light, nemesis or ally or onlooker as it was to the things that lived in the Elmever, descended upon it from the branches.

It fell lightly, in fact beautifully, like a dropped scrap of silk: pale lavender gray, stitched all over with roses and vines in silvery thread. In its grace it seemed weightless, hungerless, and for a terrible moment Veris thought, as the unicorn pivoted toward her and the boy, that she had failed.

She thought: *I should move my hand so he can scream; and I should cover his eyes so he does not see this.*

But she couldn't move; and, a moment later, nor could the unicorn. It flinched, bucked, snarled at first, then began to howl, as the floating thing sank into it, inexorable, still softly glowing, and began to feed.

The boy's heart hammered against Veris's chest, hard enough to make the brass buckles jingle against each other. Ten paces away, the girl watched, stunned, through the trees. The unicorn thrashed, kicked, could not dislodge its tormentor; the great horn swept through the air, all to no avail. The ground trembled as it stamped and whirled, but without hands, it could not get the thing off its back.

Was it distracted enough? Veris could not tell. And in some fashion, it did not even matter; they must go, and quickly. The day burned on like a match toward the fingertips. She released Aram, and beckoned to Eleonor, and when they three were together again, she took both their hands and they ducked low and ran, heedless of the whips and slaps of the branches against their faces.

$\sim$

Aram sobbed softly as he walked, but Veris could spare no time to comfort him; from the corner of her eye she watched as Eleonor also did not, only put her arm around his shoulder and wound her fingers into a loose spot under the golden braid and fur that trimmed his shoulder, as if this was an accustomed place for her hand to go. And Veris, who had been an only child, and far distant from her cousins, felt something like envy: for this wordless love, when it would have been so easy for them to destroy one another in a moment of weakness as children often did. Aram was stockier and stronger than Eleonor, though shorter for now; he probably weighed more than she did, Veris gauged, looking at the girl's slender build. In a few years he would tower over her, but he would still do as she told him, he would still wish to be her, he would hang upon her every word. Had they learned this tenderness from their father? It could not be.

At any rate, it was none of Veris's business. They had learned obedience too, and she was grateful. Her tokens squirmed minutely in her clenched fist, but she disregarded them for now; they must get away from the worst of the woods at least a little while, if they could. Time was so precious, but life more precious still; they could not escape late but they *must* escape alive.

She took them uphill, meaning to find the mountains she had seen last time, which seemed both very far and very near from the village itself, an optical illusion that the residents were used to, and ignored. The only time it was mentioned generally was when nobles were around for any length of time; and then you had to warn them against trying for a day trip to the mountains, as there was something unpleasant about time and distance there.

No one said *magic* and no one said *Stay out of the*

woods. It didn't always work. But the place where the mountains met the trees was the strongest portion of the border between the Elmever and the real forest, and also, it seemed, the place where the two places fought their shared space the hardest. Whatever the real reason, the creatures avoided it, which made heading there worth it to Veris.

Nothing more seemed to pursue them as they climbed higher, as the trees thinned out, the light became paler, and the ground stonier. But there also were no birds, and no insects, and the air itself grew listless and insubstantial as the light. A sickly mist blew about at shin-level, hiding the mats of colorless leaves, fallen twigs gray rather than brown or green. It felt as if life was being bled from the world. Veris felt it all over her skin like splashes of cold water; the children were silent, not weeping nor speaking.

She thought: *They love their father truly, but obedience also is in them, and fear.*

For no reason she also thought of the wolves she had seen when she had entered the woods. Skinny, their forepaws so narrow under the fur they looked like human wrists. Her own wrists, perhaps.

I am no adventurer, no warrior, no soldier. The Tyrant should have sent some giant in his employ. With sword and fire.

Ah, but the giant would never have returned.

You could light fires in the north woods, in those first ten or twelve paces before you risked entering the other place; but nothing burned, not really. Not out of control. Something in there smothered it at once: then retaliated. There were stories from hundreds of years ago. Then through the natural and subtle processes of self-selection the population of the valley had been bred to never light a fire in there again.

"It smells better here," Eleonor whispered to Veris when they paused. "Don't you think?"

"Yes."

"Does that mean we're getting . . . out?"

"I'm afraid it doesn't."

Eleonor sighed, and sipped sparingly of her canteen: *Good girl,* Veris thought automatically. For you dared eat or drink nothing in here, and they would be out of the water they had brought soon. Aram's head was nodding; he leaned against his sister and closed his eyes. Veris envied him for a moment: a nap here of all places safe, watched by two others. Young children badly needed their sleep, she knew. Would go from running about to dropping on the spot. But he must awaken and walk again soon.

"Nothing's what it seems to be in here," said Veris.

Eleonor nodded, glanced down at Aram's shiny,

slumped head, glanced back. "I believe you," she said. "Because when we first got lost . . . I mean, we had only been walking a few minutes. It was dark, but we had brought candles, you know. From our chamber. And we saw . . . faces, people . . ."

She fell silent for a moment, tried again. "We saw someone we used to know. Or who looked like him: a groom who used to work in the courtyard stables, Sibunu his name was. And Aram called out to him. You know. Because he forgot, I suppose . . ."

"Forgot what?"

"That Sibu is dead," Eleonor said matter-of-factly. "His head was put up in the throne room. Father had him killed. Anyway it was about two winters ago . . . maybe three, I don't remember. But see, Aram loved him because he used to take him out on the ponies, secretly, sometimes, because Father said he was too young to learn to ride . . . it doesn't matter. He didn't come toward us, he just looked at us and then ran away.

"And when he did I saw . . . well, it wasn't him. I mean, of course it wasn't him, and I already knew it couldn't be. But it *really wasn't*. It was something else, like a . . . like a deer, only not quite, and made of wood, only not really. I don't know. And made to look like Sibu. And as it moved . . . it did look like him, perfectly, but then it didn't, but then it did, but then it didn't again. I had to grab Aram before he ran after the thing. I didn't want to lose him in the darkness. And of course I dropped my candle . . ."

Her face crumpled, and now, at last, Veris thought, there would be tears; but the girl pushed them away again, and took a long, shaky breath. She was shivering, her clothes like all of their clothes soaked with sweat and mist; even the deep brown of her eyes seemed emptied of color, and the dark wings of her brows above them. "Father told us magic was real," she whispered. "But he said we'd never see it, not here . . . that he had put his castle here because it was safe, because the rest of the empire was full of these awful things. Sorcerers and necromancers and witches and wizards."

"What's a necromancer?"

"Oh, they bring people back from the dead," she said, wiping her nose with her velvet sleeve. "He said. I don't think they're real. Or, well . . ." She looked around them; they had gained some height, and managed to put a flat, smooth slab of grainy stone at their backs; from here, below and above them, the woods still stretched, brimming and burning with magic like an invisible fire. If you did not believe in magic, a day here would teach you to believe, like it or no. You were surrounded by it, and must guard yourself against it, this thing you did not believe in.

"What do you do when you're not doing this?"

Eleonor said after a few minutes.

"I'm rarely doing this," Veris said severely. "And I certainly wouldn't be, if you two had shown an ounce of common sense. At any rate: I sell vegetables, if you must know. And I breed and sell rabbits and rabbit products; and I read and write letters for the village."

"They pay you money for that? Can't people do it themselves?"

"No. Most of the villagers cannot. But they have family in other places in the valley and elsewhere that they would like to hear from."

"Do you have your own children?"

"No. Children are very troublesome things."

Eleonor laughed for the first time, then looked down at Aram again. "When we get back," she said, "I think I'll write a book about this."

If, Veris thought. "Yes," she said, "you certainly should. Raise him up, please; we'll have a few bites of food, and then we must keep going."

As they ate, Veris continued to scan the stones and branches around them for birds to ask for directions; it wasn't necessarily that she thought they could be trusted to know, but they were not like the people and other beasts in here, and there was no magic about them, nor glamour, alone, she thought, out of all the living things in this place. But there was nothing.

Perhaps they had all been frightened away by the commotion with their pursuer; or perhaps they simply did not like this place near the mountains, an in-between place in a place already made of in-between places, where there was nothing to eat and even the most featherlight song would fall leaden to the ground.

"Hello? Hello?"

Veris leapt to her feet, scattering bits of bread and apple core, her hand up as if she held a weapon, which she did not. Out of the mist crept two gangrel things that for a moment she mistook as animals: something slinking and hungry, a weasel or a stoat or a snake. But as they approached, meek, heads down, they seemed only to be children, and real ones at that, with none of the slight but unsettling differences of the people who lived in the forest.

Still, her heart hammered; still, she resolved to say nothing unless they spoke again. Aram and Eleonor arrayed themselves on either side of her, astonished but unmoving. The newcomers were ragged, and each wore only a brief skirt or loincloth of dead leaves clumsily tied together with vining plants, like a scrap of dirty canvas. They were similarly brown of skin, and one had dark hair and one light, and the hair was long and matted and unclean; they did not seem particularly related, and their faces were very different in eyes and mouth. Their ribs shone through their dirty sides.

"Who are you?" Aram blurted, and Eleonor shushed him a moment too late.

The children glanced at one another, as if conferring, then back to Veris. "We have no names now," the darker-haired child said; their voice was breathy, but still struck Veris as human. "We will be given new ones."

"By whom?" Veris said.

"Our mother and father," the other child said. "When the time is right. They said."

"Don't they give you food?" Aram said, and Eleonor, fed up, snapped "Shush!" and pulled him to her roughly, hissing something in his ear. He whimpered, and fell silent.

"Yes," said the first child. "We eat. Only . . ."

In the pause, Veris studied their faces, what she could see of them through the dirt. They had no names; but did they not, somewhat, resemble a few of the children she still saw playing around the village? Particularly the combination of that brown skin with that light, curly hair; the valley had been invaded again and again, resettled by merchants and armies and hunters and nomads, and because of the emigration and immigration from a hundred places there was no "look" to the valley, and none to the village, but Veris was a keen observer of faces. These were not known to her, but had an undeniable familiarity, like echoes. Very like the Berrymans, and the Mosses? No? But the last child lost to either family had been long before her time, even before her grandfather's time, and . . .

"They will come to find us soon," the first child said. "To give us food. You could come with us . . . be a family . . ."

Their dirty faces tightened when it was spoken, and Veris could only imagine how often they had both heard that during their time here. *We're a family. Us, we're a family. You had no family before us.*

They had come in here by accident, probably not at the same time, and never gone back out, and their deaths had been mourned with the standard ceremony and funeral, and they had been . . . adopted, no, abducted, and had never aged, and had been here all this time . . .

Veris shuddered, then focused on the first part of the child's statement rather than the last; she had no desire to be here when the children's abductors came looking for them. "Then we will leave you to it," she said. "We do not wish to interrupt your meal. We will go."

"Come with us," they both whispered, rising from their squats, reaching out to Veris, showing her their empty hands as if to reassure her that, like her, they held no weapons. Their palms were crisscrossed with a hundred ridged horizontal scars, thin and white as the tendrils of a root.

"We are leaving," Veris said. She held a hand out without looking, and felt Eleonor take it; and hoped, as she carefully began to descend, edging away from the other children, that the girl had taken her brother's hand too. Eleonor's hand in hers was ice-cold, and soaked with sweat. Would it be better if the children that came into this place truly died? Some probably had, Veris thought, or hoped. Because if you didn't, and instead the people here took you in, it might seem like a mercy, but . . .

She paused, some steps downslope; already the intervening underbrush, bright leaves of yellow and fluttering amber and red, obscured the children except for their heads. They had not moved, and still stared at the place where she had been. "Come with *us*," she said softly. "We are getting out of here. You could come with us."

"No!" whispered Eleonor.

Aram said nothing, but Veris felt his eyes on her: large, hopeful.

The children wavered, but did not move. "We are very happy here," said the lighter-haired one. "We have a family."

Veris stared at the child, at the higgledy-piggledy mouth of any ordinary child, milkteeth and marriage-teeth still not in their final places, and at the tendons that stood out along the child's neck, and again at the exposed collarbones, the thinness of the shoulders. It might have been a hundred years, two hundred. Living forever. Wasting away. "We could find you a new family," Veris said, hearing her voice tremble at the pity of it all. "In the village. Don't you remember the village?"

Silence. They did not move. A light, chill breeze sprang up, sweet with leaf and soil.

"It's almost harvest," Veris said. "The grass is still green. The grapes are fat. You could have a bed again. Names again. Come with us."

"Please," whispered Aram.

"No," the darker-haired boy finally said. "No. We are very happy here. We have a family. All the children are happy here."

Veris's blood ran cold: she wished the child had not said *all*. How many, how very many, children were here . . . how many adults had come in, grown men and women, had perished instead? And what had happened to anyone either old or young if they had not been "adopted" by the creatures here?

No, it was better to not know; everything she had learned here she regretted learning. She felt it burrow into her mind and under her ribs like a worm, all this knowledge. Poisoned, venomous. Squirming. Not dead.

"You will not come?" she said, for the last time: three and three and three, she had not realized until she asked that she had asked three times.

They would not come. And what held them there was not love; and at this point, after so long, it was barely fear. Something was dead inside of them, something had been killed, and buried deep, under their gleaming ribs. Now they had an existence rather than a life. Might that thing come back to life in the village? Veris hoped so, but she could not compel them, though her heart might break.

At last she turned her back upon them, and she and Eleonor and Aram hurried softly through the woods, through a gentle pattering storm of golden leaves. Had the light changed? Was night on its way, in its silver chariot, drawn by the four celestial boar? A children's story, but the speed of it: that was more terrifying than any stray children or their guardians in this entire forest. And in here you could not see the crescent moon of the leader's tusk anyway...

She did not know how long they stumbled along, only that her hip and shoulder hurt more and more, and no longer bled but only ached and stabbed her deep inside; only that it became harder and harder to climb over the roots, and more difficult to lift or pull one or another child over the stones and across the ruts and hollows; more than once they heard beasts nearby, grunting and snuffling, and they turned from their way, and had to stop and consult the tokens again, when they chose to speak.

They were close; they must be close to a way out. It did not have to be near the castle, she whispered to the cube, the chestnut, the boar that seemed to huddle close for safety on her filthy palm. It did not! Truly. Wherever it was, so long as it led out of here, she would be happy, grateful, she would build a shrine to them in her room, no matter how long the walk.

She was tired, she whispered to the things, and so were the children, and she was fearful of making mistakes—of misinterpreting their twitches and subtle shifts of weight. "Please," she murmured. "Just a few hours more. We're so tired. We cannot fail now."

"Can I talk to them?" Aram whispered, clinging to her elbow.

"If you like." She lowered the hand, where the tokens had been unmoving for some minutes, to his level. All around them the leaves and branches clattered, then went still.

"Are we going the right way?" Aram did not quite dare to touch them, but he brought his face close to them, to eye level, so that his eyelashes brushed her hand. Eleonor snorted in disdain, but watched as closely as he, keeping one hand absently on his shoulder, as if he might bolt.

The tokens did not move; Veris had not expected them to, and had been humoring the child because he was tired, and so was she.

"Oh well," Eleonor said. "Let's—"

"Are we going the *wrong* way?" Aram added, his breath hot on her fingers.

All three items moved at once: and away from each other, all in a different direction, leaving clear trails scratched in the dirt and dried blood. Aram gasped; Veris glared at the things. An unhelpful answer, and they had done this last time, too, hadn't they?

But last time it had meant something like: *Be on your guard.*

And she hadn't realized it till the moment that their final adversary had come after them, and had almost gotten within reach of its horn, and . . .

Veris shook her head sharply, as if the memory might dislodge itself from her ear and break on the ground like a cup, losing its power. But they were certainly going the wrong way, because when she brought her head back around, the woods surrounding them—beech and elm, oak and maple mixed—had dissolved, and they stood at the edge of a grassy clearing bordered all around with dark silky pines that met overhead in a kind of cathedral, letting in only darting rays of the long amber light.

Flame flared: the familiar pop and hiss of an ordinary lucifer, and a faint, homey whiff of sulfur. And candles burned abruptly in golden candelabra, three-pronged, and three of them (of course, she thought: because all the world is a fable), along a table laid with thick white cloth, woven with infinite minute traceries of golden thread. In shape and form this so closely resembled one of the flying creatures that Veris simply froze in place; and it must have reminded the children of the same thing, for they did not step forward, despite the table's contents: a dozen silver dishes uncovered, clear glass bottles of wine and water, and three places set with glimmering cutlery.

"It's not real," Veris said calmly, watching the candle-flames dance on the polished surface of the spoons. "And we do not eat the food in here. Not one bite. Not one sip."

"Not one," said Eleonor.

"Not one," said Aram.

"Not even one?" said a voice, and from the darkness at the far end of the table stepped a tall man who looked like a fox, or a fox that looked like a man; from certain angles he seemed to give the effect of the landscape itself, that of a folded piece of paper which should not, but did, somehow display the entire drawing, including the portion of it inside the fold.

He had too much face, and then again not enough; he had a tail, but of course he did not, he wore a dark red frock-coat like the singers that came to the fairs, and its cutaway tails gave the effect. He definitely wore a broad-brimmed hat tied with a dove-gray ribbon so long it brushed against the backs of his calves as he moved. And he certainly had very white and even teeth.

"Why, the whole place is alive with tales of your tres-pass," he said; a plate materialized under his paw, or his hand, in its rust-colored kidskin glove. "Aren't you three little lost mice hungry? Come along, I know *you* are. Strapping young man as you are. There's a lovely ham. Look."

Aram shook his head, though his stomach audibly called out, as did Veris's. But the cramping of her viscera around their few mouthfuls of food did not compare to the fear they felt below the hunger. This thing, whatever it was, this man, this not-man, was very *good*: his voice sounded nearly human. She truly had to concentrate to hear the strangeness in it: the sound of the woods, of wind blowing over broken branches, deep in his chest, and the way he snipped off the ends of his words like trimming the buds from a rosebush.

"Or there's a lovely fish with lemons," the fox went on; he hummed, walked along the table, filling his plate. "Come come, young lady. You like fish, I know you do. And how often do those silly villagers even see a lemon? Those come from warmer climes. Do you know how many miles you have to go before a lemon can grow?"

"Then where did you get one?" Eleonor said skepti-cally. Veris hissed at her to be quiet, chuckling under her breath; it wasn't funny, really, nor was the fox-man's glare, and they were still in mortal danger, because in here you never weren't, but she did have a point.

The fish was lovely, because it could be nothing but; longer than Veris's outstretched arm, scales silverypink as a winter dawn, the lemon slices sparkling like suns against the clouds of dense white meat. Eleonor looked at it with real longing, warring with her common sense. But neither child moved from her side. At their feet even the smell of the grass rose, and made their mouths water.

"No," Veris said. "We will not. Leave us, so that we can continue home."

"But you will never go home," the fox-man said. "Be reasonable. Everyone knows you are here. I suppose that means nothing to you. To us it means . . ." He paused, theatrically, and slid his knife into a golden roast chicken, bristling with herbs and fried onions. "Well. Fresh meat. For one. But also that our borders are growing weak, our walls are crumbling . . . or else you would not have come even so far. Hm? Simply by breathing our air for this long you have declared yourself our enemy."

"We've done no such thing."

"And *these* two. Hm. Newcomers to the land: they lack our smell. I suppose their father will come in here, hmm? With his legions and legions and legions. To teach us a lesson."

"No," Veris said. "He won't."

"You would vouch for him? You, his guarantor?"

"No."

"Pity." The fox-man sat with his brimming plate and poured himself a glass of violet-red wine, through which the candle-flames shone like stained glass. "I hear he has some quite amazing vintages in his cellars. Along with other things . . ."

"It's not real," Veris murmured. "None of it. It isn't real."

Eleonor nodded; Aram stared, and whimpered, a little involuntary noise he did not seem aware that he had made.

The fox lowered his snout and lapped at the pooling sauces on the plate; the man cleaved pieces of fish, and placed the golden fork into his mouth; and both happened at once, which gave Veris a headache to watch. She stared down at the grass, each blade as thick as a ribbon. "It only looks real," she said, as much to the children as to herself. "He isn't really eating."

"No? You say I am not?" The fox-man chuckled, and licked his lips lingeringly, and pushed aside his plate. "Well. Believe what you like. Hm? I am not here to proselytize."

"What are you here for?" Veris said evenly.

"Why, to size you up," he said. "To make your

measure . . . one greater than me, you know, is very in-terested in your progress this time. Not my business to know why. I suppose because you are interesting people. Hm?" He laughed.

"To delay us," Veris said. "To lose us further in the Elmever."

He started. "So! You have wisdom as well as Knowl-edge. Well. In another place, another time, we might have been friends; we could have talked long and wise. But here, well, we cannot, I suppose you understand. Play a game with me and I'll let you leave alive. And not spitted and roasted with rare spices."

"No."

"What kind of game?" blurted Aram, and Veris, leaden with horror nearly before the words left his mouth, snatched at the boy's velvet shirt too late to catch him; Eleonor made a grab for him as well that fell short, then cried out as she was dragged as if with invisible chains across the grass toward the table, from which the food and drink all suddenly vanished, leaving only the three candelabra and their white pillars under the arching trees like the upthrust antlers of deer.

And the white tablecloth, so thick and so sinisterly embroidered with its veins of gold, was also gone; and beneath it was something darkly stained, a pale gray gran-ite marked all over with black, and it did not make Veris think of food anymore, but other things, older, crueler. A thousand invasions had diluted the religions of the valley, filling it with tiny gods and household spirits only half-believed and intermittently worshipped or blamed; but there had been *something* believed here once, and with absolute conviction.

She strained against the invisible wall that held her from the children, and felt things grind and catch inside her, and cried out, in vain, and heard how faint it was, and saw how their heads did not turn.

Would the fox-thing harm them? She did not think he was permitted to; but it also did not matter. He could harm *her*, and the children would never get out on their own. Veris hammered on the unseen barrier, to no avail.

His voice came to her businesslike, crisp as a dry leaf. "A very simple game. With dice. You see? I took these from a traveler long ago, so very long ago, inside these woods . . . he played and he lost and I took my prize."

"What would you take from us if we lose?" Eleonor said. In the darkness her face was more than white; it was ghostly, like chalkdust.

"Oh, I don't know," the fox-man said indulgently. "What have you got? I like your little daggers; but I have fangs and claws. I smell matches in your bag; we always need matches, you know. Or perhaps I will take your names again . . . names are such delicious things, even second-hand. Or . . ."

He pretended to stare up at the interlaced branches above them, thinking; he rattled the black dice in his paw and his gloved hand. "Or perhaps your favorite memory of your brother. Or some perfect spring days. Not too many: eight or ten. Or . . . something else."

Eleonor watched him, eyes wide; Aram's face was the picture of regret. Seven years old, Veris thought distractedly: he had resisted so much, and as best as he could, but he had slipped up, and they were losing precious time. If the children refused to play, the fox would simply wait them out, like any ambush predator; if they did play, they would lose. The second way might be a swifter defeat; or, she hoped, a success.

"*I* will play!" shouted Veris through the wall of the enchantment, and found that she could move her arms, her legs, of a sudden, though they were sore. She stumbled to the grass, rose, and half-ran to the stone platform, hitting her knee sharply on the chair that materialized out of the ground between the two children, who watched her in horror. "I will play. Instead of them. And I can give you something, supposing I lose; and you must give me something I choose, supposing I win. Do we have an agreement?"

"Oh, how canny!" The fox chuckled coyly, and began to put away his dice, into what was both clearly a fold in his russet fur and a slim pocket in his morning coat. "Then we shall play with cards, since you are no child, and can count higher than six."

Veris reached out and stopped just before touching him. Her fingertips trembled an inch shy of his clean hide; he stared at them disdainfully. "No, we will play what you would have played with them," she said, keeping her voice steady. "We will play their game. And I will play in their stead."

"But you are a tricksy one!" The fox smiled, and took out the dice again, placing them on the stained gray granite, all in a row, one two three. "Stories are still told of your last exploit here . . . so long ago that no one believed you would come back. Certainly many believed you had perished since."

"I know of your beliefs," Veris said.

"And some even said," he added, toying with the dice, as his unfriendly, reddish-brown eyes gazed into hers, "that we should declare your life forfeit at once, should you ever be foolish enough to return. Place a bounty upon your head."

"A bounty!" Veris found herself both alarmed and slightly flattered by the notion, and intensely wished, too, that she had never agreed to return; let the Tyrant simply kill her there in the throne room, let his great white bony hand throttle out her life. She should not be here; she should not have been here the first time; these woods were not meant for mortals. But she was a sensible woman, and knew she must play this little game before the fox-man would let her play the real one. "I cannot imagine what could be paid as a bounty for my head. Nor by whom."

"But you are an imaginative creature," the fox said. "Surely."

They smiled at each other: a mere baring of teeth. Veris could no longer smell even a hint of the food that had seemed so ravishingly luscious a minute ago; but she could smell the acerbic breath of the trees, and the sweetness of the beeswax candles, and the smell of the fox, or his clothes: slightly gamey, like a pheasant hung too long.

Veris let his words hang in the air, drift off, find other listeners. In the trunks of the pines, she spotted two small gleaming sets of eyes, and felt no fear, only sadness: the two ragged children they had seen before, watching her with a kind of silent, starving desperation. Whether they had reported Veris's movements on purpose or by accident, Veris could not fault them. Even after a century they were still children.

And again she thought: *Monsters, the children of monsters. But innocent. You do not inherit what you are born to; and you do not inherit your own theft.*

Their innocence will not save them from harm. And it has not. Still it must be remembered.

"One game," Veris said to the fox.

"Two," said the fox. "As I wished to play with each of your young friends. The boy first. Then the girl."

"But if two," Veris said, "then what if we come to a draw? It should be one. Or three."

The fox lifted his lip over a white canine, his white whiskers, or moustache, sparkling in the candlelight. Under Veris's hands the stone seemed to grow colder, paler, the stains upon it darker. The fox, she knew, had had plans for two games; there had been some little enchantment, some little cheat, planned for them. By asking for one or three, Veris had spoiled something. She was sure it was very small, but he was piqued nonetheless. She did not let herself feel anything resembling hope.

"Two," said the fox. "It will not come to a draw."

So you admit you will cheat? she almost said, but said instead, "Very well. Tell me about your game."

"Oh, very simple." He nudged the three dice toward her: very old they seemed, and carved out of some naturally black wood. Their dots were painted rather than incised, and glimmered faintly, not quite silvery, more like the phosphorescence of fishbones. Veris could see why the fox had taken them as his prize. They were lovely, and looked heavy and satisfying to the hand.

He said, "A game for children. You can both count, can't you?" He flicked a wink at them, and Eleonor visibly flinched. "You say evens, I say odds, or you say odds, and I say evens, and whichever roll has more of them wins the game. I roll, then you roll. For fairness."

"I have never known the residents here to be overoccupied with fairness," Veris said.

"Some of us are less so," the fox allowed. "But you mustn't judge us all on their trespasses, my dear. Come now. I will roll. Evens or odds?"

"Evens," said Veris.

He lifted his gloved hand, and the dice fell the few inches to the granite and clattered and spun: a three, and a two, and a five.

"You lose," said the fox.

"My turn," said Veris. The children in their velvet wavered in the corner of her eyes, as if they were on the verge of dissolving; she saw them there like clouds, one in dark violet, and one in dark blue, and their hair as black as the wings of crows. Innocent. Take them back to their monster; do not let them fall to these ones.

She picked up the three dice and shook them gently in both hands. "Evens or odds?"

He fluttered his dark lashes at her. "Now I will say evens."

"So I say odds," Veris said, and dropped them upon the

granite. A one, and a three ... and a blank.

The fox stared long at the little cube of coal, and the hackles upon his neck, or his long ginger hair, raised, so that for just a moment Veris imagined him lunging across the table at her, white teeth fastening into her throat ... but at last he laughed uproariously, rocking back on the delicate legs of his chair. "Oh! A lady after my own heart. Very much a lady after my own heart. Well, it seems that I lose."

"So we have a draw," Veris said, returning his dice and taking back her token. "I did warn you this might happen."

"So you did. So you did," he chuckled, wiping his eyes. "What shall we do now? Supposing we both give each other something. For we have both won; and we have both lost."

"Let the children go, and we can have a conversation."

The fox waved his hand extravagantly, and the candle-flames guttered, and Eleonor and Aram fell with a gasp to the grass, rose, stood on either side of Veris's chair. For a moment there was no sound but their hitching breath and the crackle of the candles.

"Give me something nice," the fox-man said, leaning forward, "and I will show you a short-cut out. You do not have enough time to walk all the way back from whence you came."

"A short-cut? That does not seem very likely," Veris said mildly.

"It does not, does it?" the fox agreed, and whistled sharply through his teeth. From the trees slunk something small, furred, a slightly greasy sheen around it, like the glow around ships on certain stormy nights.

It was a brown rat, or something made to look like a rat, Veris corrected herself automatically; and it wore a tiny collar of carven wood, knotted and locked in the back behind its ears by a thin rope of woven vines, with a dead leaf sprouting from it here and there. The rope trailed behind it several feet, into the darkness. It glanced up at Veris, at the fox, then hung its head and waited in the grass. "My servant here would be happy to show you the way," the fox said. "Personally. Step by step."

"And why would you be so eager to see us gone from your realm, good sir?"

"Eager? Certainly not. But a deal is a deal. Or rather, it could be if you pay me what I ask."

"And what do you ask of me?" Veris felt her pulse in her wrists against the cold stone, and she slowly withdrew her hands from the fox's sight, and placed them calmly in her lap, against the blood-stiffened cloth of her breeches. Without quite meaning to, they knotted themselves into a fist.

Time, time, time, said her heartbeat. Time, time. From

the mountainous border where they had unwisely rested she had seen the same thing as the children, and drawn the same conclusion, though none of them had spoken it aloud: to turn one way, or another, was hundreds of miles of the same wood; you could not go "the long way" out of Elmever. You had to go through. And it was a fact that there *were* hidden ways to go through that had nothing to do with distance.

She had been lucky enough to trade for one last time, but this was not last time, and what she had then was now gone. The creatures here knew the ways; she did not.

"I would like your worst memory," said the fox-man, and he was all fox now, six feet tall, black-lipped, hungry, smiling, round-eyed. His claws scraped against the stone. "Your worst, your very worst. I would like to eat . . . it . . . up."

Veris did not move. "And for this, you would let us have the use of your guide, to show us the way out of the Elmever? To return us to our world safe, and alive, and ourselves?"

"Yes, yes." Not hungry for it, she thought, looking at his open mouth. Rabid for it. She thought: *One nip.*

But he would not nip her. He wanted something much tastier against his silken pink tongue. The rat, sensibly, backed away from his paws as they scrabbled in the grass.

"The death of my father," she said.

"More."

Bile rose in her throat like the lick of a flame. "Mama died quickly, as it happened. Very quickly. The Tyrant's soldiers had something . . . I don't remember what they called it. They would roll it at the enemy and then run off, and it would explode like a piece of hollow coal in the fire. But bigger, much bigger. So violent . . ."

The trees seemed to fade, and all around she saw what she had seen then, even though she had arrived at the end, not at the beginning, of her mother's death. Such was the power of this place, she knew, but it was too real for her to look away from; there were no shadows a moment ago but now there were shadows, real and dark, and there was depth, height, mass, there was light and color, and noise.

She raised her voice against the sounds of war. "She was very close to one. Not to the fighters—not to the fighting, I mean. She was standing behind a stone wall. It did not save her. She died at once. And six other people from the valley. All in a moment. She was trying to get eggs. For me and my father. All our chickens had been taken by the Tyrant's armies.

"But my father . . . after she died, he wouldn't eat. I thought he was trying to save what we had for me. So I went out and . . . I got us food. However I could. From whoever. Even from the Tyrant's men, sometimes. They had better supplies by then, compared to the rest of the valley, because they were getting supply wagons from the south and the east . . ."

"More, more. How did you get food? Tell me how." The fox's saliva spilled onto the table and pooled there, viscous and vile.

"Not in front of the children," Veris said.

"Tell me how! Tell me! The worst, you claim. You claim the worst. We have ways of knowing whether you speak truth. Now *tell me!*" he screamed.

Aram and Eleonor both cried out involuntarily at the high scream of the fox, which perhaps they had never heard from the castle (no, of course not: the dogs would frighten them off, and they would never hear that terrible noise at night, the too-human shrieks and wails). Veris unbound her hands from one another and, under the table, moved them to take the children's hands.

"I was twelve. I believed I was old enough to do what I did with my body," she said steadily. "And so did the soldiers. They didn't ask, anyway, and if they would have asked I knew they wouldn't care. And soon I didn't care that they didn't care. Papa didn't ask either. I came home bleeding from front and back a few times, and it showed on my dress, and he didn't ask. But he did stop eating. And I begged him to eat, I screamed at him. I thought about forcing the food into his mouth. I was bigger than him by then, stronger. Which wasn't hard. He had never been a big man."

"Yes, yes," the fox hissed greedily. "Yes, terrible."

"But he didn't. He insisted *I* eat. Even when there was food for both of us. Even when I showed him. Then he got sick, of course he did. And I was so angry. I blamed him. Then I blamed myself: I hadn't gotten the right things, I hadn't gotten healthy food for him, good food. I must have given him something bad and it made him sick..."

"And he died. Oh, awful. Was it a bad death? Very bad?"

"The worst I had ever seen," Veris said, and she looked around at the interior of their house, the old house, with its red brick walls and the tiled fireplace, and her father no longer in his chair but slid out of it and lying on the hearth, mindless of the embers that occasionally spat into his hair and beard.

"He was in pain, and for a while he said nothing, and then he stopped being able to say nothing: he screamed and moaned in his sleep, and then after a while in his waking too, and we had no doctors, our doctors were all dead, and he screamed and screamed till he lost his voice, and then a month after that he died. I found him... I found him outside... in the grass. Half-frozen. His mouth all full of snow and ice. As if he had been eating it to soothe the fire inside . . ."

"Beautiful," whispered the fox, and tapped his paws on the stone. "And you call us monsters in here. Well, we do not, ourselves, recognize the word."

"But you do monstrous things," Veris said, and the room faded around her, and the trees returned, black and thick as fur. "I have seen them . . ."

"Once or twice," said the fox airily, dropping to all fours. "Here or there. We do not make a *habit* of it. And you, speaking of monstrous, the whole forest is talking about it: you killed a guardian!"

"It was already dead!"

"It clearly was not; it was moving about."

There was no sense wasting time arguing with him; Veris shakily pushed her chair back from the altar, and looked down at the enormous fox slavering into the grass, the rat cowering in the shadow of the stone. "Give me the rope, and let us go. I have paid you."

"O, you paid. Here." The fox balanced on three paws, and slapped at the thin rope with his fourth; Veris stooped and quickly seized it, and wrapped it twice around her hand.

"Goodbye," said Veris, turning from him; the rat scampered ahead of her, limping, and she felt sorry for it; she hoped the fox had not been maltreating it, in whatever form he had taken. "And I hope I never see you again."

"What an unladylike thing to hope," the fox said, and vanished, along with the stone altar and his cathedral of trees, leaving them back in the dim, golden cavern of the woods once more: much dimmer, Veris realized with alarm. Perceptibly dimmer now, when it should have been painfully bright after the darkness of the fox's dining room.

"Hurry," Veris said, to the rat, to herself, to the children. "Hurry, hurry."

~

Now they did not speak as they ran after the rat; they only went quickly for a while, over the more even ground, then slowed, as it scurried up and over obstacles that they had to climb or scramble over, into a deepening gloom. *Your father killed my father,* Veris had said, and the children had heard her say it, and they said nothing.

She had not expected sympathy or apologies; they were too young. And Eleonor, the heir, would have to grow up and kill, yes, fathers, mothers, brothers, sisters, everybody, and her father the Tyrant would be raising her up to get used to the idea; perhaps, Veris thought, the girl had already been to interrogations, to executions, to trials, to decimations; perhaps she had seen whole squadrons of their own soldiers killed in front of her, as legend said the Tyrant would sometimes do randomly when an area had been too slow in the conquering, or when there had been whispers of sedition.

Eleonor would be raised to believe that there were people you could become attached to, and people you could not; and even at her age, Veris suspected she was training herself very competently to separate them in her mind, and not to allow people from one category to enter the other. And Veris knew where she would fall in this: no attachment; a useful servant; sent to help us, as the other servants are.

"Hurry," she breathed, because it was all she could say. Or: "Lift your left leg, and I will pull." Or: "No, not that way. Here: over the log."

And on top of everything else it began to rain: lightly at first, so that it seemed only that the smell of incoming rain had penetrated into the forest from the far edge of the storm, then heavier, so that it seemed it rained nearby but only the damp of it reached them, and then in minutes it became sensible, and then it fell in chill torrents that soaked them to the skin.

"Are we allowed to drink the rain?" Aram whispered, miserably wiping his face.

"I don't know," Veris said. "But I've already swallowed some, so if there's a curse in it, then we're all cursed together."

He smiled uncertainly at her, though it fell away at once. "I'm sorry I was stupid," he said. "Back there, with the . . . man . . . and his game."

"You don't need to apologize. And you weren't."

"Leo said I was."

"It was a cruel thing to say," Veris said. Aram nodded, and seemed again about to speak, then put his head down and trudged on next to her; and on her other side, Veris was not sure that Eleonor had heard anything they had said, the rain was so loud.

If there was one blessing, it was that there was no path through the woods, which would have turned to an impassable mire in minutes; instead the moss and lichen, roots and bark, branches and leaves funneled the water away to their secret places, leaving slicks and hollows but no disastrous bogs. The sole kindness of the forest was that it remained untouched and able to do so, Veris reflected; if this same rain was falling on the south woods (which she doubted) it would be knee-deep in mud.

Say nothing, she told herself. *We're so close. Get them out, get them home.*

Get them out. Get them home.

Get them away from me. Back to their own kind.

On the end of its lead, the rat snuffled, paused, turned back to look at her with an expression so plainly human that she squatted down, painfully, and cocked her ear to listen to it speak. But it said nothing, and only looked ahead of it, then back at her: urgently, and the rain slicking down its fur so that it looked half its size, just like you would say of a wet child that they resembled a drowned rat, and almost Veris wanted to apologize for having eaten so many of its kind during the war. But anyway those were village rats, not wood ones. Perhaps they did not know each other.

Her mind was wandering again; she shook her head and stood, looking at where the rat was indicating; the ground was crisscrossed with fallen branches and even young saplings, and now she could hear the source of the rat's worry: running water, low and menacing over the sound of the rain.

"Wait here," Veris said to the children, and stepped forward cautiously, her hands out for balance. She climbed the shifting stack of wooden debris, slick and ungainly and moving dangerously under her weight, and peered down: yes, the rain had scoured away some ancient channel, not even a streambed, perhaps just a low spot, for it was wide and moving fast, but the startlingly deep water was also crammed with leaves and sticks and mud. It churned and roared past like a carriage pulled by an infinite number of horses, heavy with the built-up water draining from the higher spots of the woods, like the flash floods that had happened while the castle was being built and before the grass had grown back.

Was there anywhere to cross? She cursed under her breath. Nothing within visible distance. But: all this wood. And the rat tugging at the leash, like a pointing dog. "All right, all right," she snarled. "You can't swim in that either, you know; there's no sense getting impatient."

All the same, impatience made her hands shake as she and the children tried to lift fallen wood that looked long enough for them to cross the stream, as it seemed to be widening by the minute; and you could not cut the trees in here, not that Veris had brought anything that could chop wood.

It was tempting though, very tempting; in her mind's eye she pictured a great heavy axe of good iron, and herself whole and fit (and about a foot taller and five stone heavier) hacking down one of these trees, any of which would easily reach across the water, so that they would not have to do this frustrating work of cobbling together a bridge that would have to be spliced together to reach.

She was exhausted, shivering, weak with hunger, and angry at herself with the knowledge that she had not brought enough food to make up for what she was burning. But the proximity to escape drove her on, the rain blurring her vision like a shawl drawn over her face, suffering innumerable tiny scratches from the rough wood.

For a moment only she allowed herself to be irritated

that the woods could take as much of her blood as they liked, while she was not permitted to take even a drop of theirs; it wasn't fair, nothing in here was fair. That was how it worked. No different without than within.

Only that without was food she could eat, and people she could love. Onwards, onwards.

When their bridge was finished it was a rickety thing, and shook even from the rain falling upon it, and Veris doubled and redoubled the rat's lead around her hand so that it barely reached from her waist to the ground; one more wind around her hand and the rat would have had to dance on its hind legs to avoid being strangled.

She looked at it; it looked back, expressionless now, dripping. A tremor ran through her, though of fear or something else she could no longer tell. Perhaps it was only the cold seeping through to her bones.

"I will cross first," she said to the children. "As a test. If it does not fall under my weight, it should not under yours. Stay together. Don't take your eyes off me."

Eleonor nodded, and reached for Aram, who shook her hand off. "I'll go first," he said. "I'll make sure it's safe."

"No. You stay here. Come only after I am across."

As she edged over the crackling and creaking wood, she heard, faintly, the sounds of the girl remonstrating with him; his voice raised; hers raised again, angry, tired. Veris looked down at her hands on the dark and lichen-spotted bark. It was better than looking at the ever-faster water rushing just a few feet below, white-capped now, surly with foam and packed with flying debris that lurched from the surface of the water like upthrust spears, then sank again, disbelieving, gone. Under her it roared now as it chewed away at the wet soil, exposing visceral tangles of surprisingly bright roots: yellow, red, golden-brown.

The bridge creaked in warning, squeaked and squealed as if it were being beaten; she tried to hurry across, but moving on her hands and knees even over so short a distance could not be rushed. She took shallow, quick breaths, and coughed and spat at the rain that still fell, and ran up her nose and into her ears. Ahead of her, the rat was a dark indistinct blob, only visible in the gloom with its accompanying glow of blue.

Sharp, sweet mocking laughter fell upon her suddenly, faint above the rain as birdsong; and she looked up instinctively to see the same small angular faces she had seen when she had first come into the Elmever. For a split second she allowed herself to feel something akin to hope: they were close! It meant they were close! Here was where—

—and she just managed to fling up an arm as the log careened toward her and smashed into the bridge.

For a second she was weightless, and falling; then

weight reasserted itself, and with it, dread, seeing the two small forms behind her also toppling into the water. She had not even noticed them joining her on the bridge, had not looked back, in her pain had felt only the creaking and trembling of her own movements, not theirs; all this passed through her mind in a flash as she hit the water, and the logs and branches rained down atop her.

Chaos, confusion, a battle flung upon her of cold water and thrusting swords that stabbed at her and vanished like assassins; she thrashed her way to the far side, while the wood still floated, and gained it, clinging to the exposed roots, and reached out an arm and took Eleonor, who screamed something incoherent—perhaps in her mother tongue, for Aram was washing away, clinging to a scrap of wood, crying out for both of them in turn.

The rat was gone, paddling frantically in the water with a squeak of despair; Veris barely noticed it, and threw away the scrap of tendrils and the broken wooden collar so both her hands were free.

No! No! We're so close!

"Climb up!" she shouted into Eleonor's ear, and thrust the child at the roots of the bank. "Get to dry ground—I will get him!"

She did not pause to see whether she was being obeyed this time; a curse on them both if they did not, it did not matter now, only Aram mattered, and his cries were moving perilous fast. Veris could not even see him; she leapt back down into the crowded current and let it take her, keeping her head up.

Most of the villagers, even those who fished in the river and the few who fished in the sea, could not swim strongly; but many could swim at least a bit, and Veris stroked and kicked to catch up with him, moving as fast as she dared in the spiky water, snatched and snagged by a thousand roots and branches, through the silvery curtains of the rain seeing Aram whirl as if something beneath the water were playing with him, sink, bob again to the surface like a cork, clinging to his log, his hair across his face so he could probably not even see, crying, "Veris! Leo! Veris!"

A narrowing of the way: blocked up with wet branches like a thatch roof had fallen into the stream. Veris redoubled her efforts, and reached it moments after Aram hit it and stuck. It caved under their weights, bowing alarmingly, water already starting to pour through the makeshift dam as the logs and branches began to strike against it. She thought of this morning: had it only been this morning? a battering ram against her door.

She seized Aram's shockingly limp form around his waist and gasped for air. How to get up? The dam was breaking. *Would* break soon. She looked around desperately, treading water and crying out now and then as a log hit her, clinging with her free hand to the soaked and creaking wood.

"Here!" someone cried on the bank. "You, you again! Here!"

Veris looked up, blinking away the water that sheeted across her face: yes, he was soaked too, but she could have risen up and kissed him, taken his hand in marriage. The strange little man who had helped her earlier, if you could call it help—he who had tried to trick her with apples, had eaten of her food, traded for the way to the four-doored house.

He was throwing down not a rope but a rickety-looking, water-logged root that she doubted would bear both their weights. Nevertheless, the dam to which she clung gave one final, sickening surge, and collapsed.

Veris snatched at the root and clung to Aram with her bad arm as she clawed her way up the bank, the rocks in her satchel dragging her down, the man pulling the while, clumsily but strongly, digging into the slick mats of leaves with his clawless, lapine paws.

Even when they had stumbled several feet into the woods, onto what was undeniably dry and solid land, she could not stop shaking, so hard that her teeth clattered together; and Aram, laid upon the ground, was deathly white and without strength, though his eyes were open; his chest gurgled darkly, as if a tributary of the stream still ran through him.

Eleonor slid to her knees beside him and, for the first time all day, burst into tears.

"It's all right," Veris lied, trying to still her teeth so she could speak. "It's all right, shh. He just had a bit of a scare, that's all; he's fine." She pulled the boy's cold body upright and draped him, with difficulty, over her forearm; the stab-wound in her shoulder had broken open well and truly again, and torn even wider; she could feel it. Fresh blood soaked her sodden sweater and dripped down her wrist. "Shh. We're both fine."

She pounded the boy's back with the heel of her hand, pushing him forward so that he coughed and vomited water between his legs; his breath still rattled, water still ran from his nose and mouth. She continued for a few minutes, wheezing with the effort, till suddenly she too was overcome by lightheadedness; everything darkened around her, and she swayed and spilled to the ground, the impact bringing her around again.

Veris brushed the film of mud and decaying leaf from her face, and reached out weakly to help as the small horned man, their rescuer, knelt and put Aram's head against his wooden knee, and slapped the boy's cheeks. Aram writhed, and spat up more water; his gaze was glazed, cloudy. Almost Veris could see a storm incoming in them. Was it water alone? Or some terrible property of water in the Elmever—had he swallowed or inhaled more than was allowed, breaking some intricate rule she did not know about?

Veris fumbled out her handkerchief full of tokens, and put it into Aram's hand; his fingers clenched weakly around it. "Aram, speak," she commanded, as the man continued to jiggle the boy's velvet shoulders, trying to bring up more water. "Tell me. Do you feel them move? Do they feel hot? Cold?"

Aram moaned, and more water drooled from the side of his slackened mouth—clear, at least, rather than silty and tannic as before. "Better," the man murmured. "See. Can you breathe? No? Yes? Breathe in for me, breathe. Sing."

He was answered with a wracking fit of coughing, and the man helped him to his feet so that Aram could bend over and put his full strength, what remained, into the coughing. Eleonor finally managed to calm herself, and came to Veris's side, hesitantly, her face swollen and pink, cooled by the rain but not enough.

"It's my fault," she sobbed. "He got away from me, and he went onto the bridge. Then I had to come after him . . . we should have let you go across first."

"He's all right now," Veris said firmly, putting an arm around the girl's shaking shoulder. The pain in her side had become a warming flame, though darkness still encroached; she seemed to see the scene as through a tunnel, like the one she had passed through earlier to-day. Earlier? It had been years ago, decades, surely. But like that: darkness, fuzziness, a thousand tiny branches making a singular whole. To their rescuer, she said, "We're terribly grateful for the help. However did you find us?"

He ducked his head, patting Aram's back in an absent fashion, as if petting a cat. "I was going to put up another tree," he admitted. "Plum, I thought. Everyone likes plums. There's a clean spot near here, where an old oak walked off. I thought: Well, the stars is right. The ground'll be wet. Then I heard you shouting."

"Well. Thank you." She reeled for a moment, then smoothed her wet hair back from her face, and held out a hand for Aram. "Come on. We've lost our guide, but I think we're not far."

"Oh, you're very close!" The man pointed into the trees, where the trunks now could almost not be distin-guished in the encroaching gloom. "That way; and soon enough you'd be able to see the walls of the castle."

Eleonor gasped with relief; Veris smiled briefly at the man. "How did you know we were going back to the cas-tle and not the village?"

For a long time there was no sound but the rain on the leaves; the mocking little faces all around them withdrew, folded themselves up again, disappeared down their angles, became only the shapes of twigs and shadows once more.

"I know many things," he said softly, and his voice was very different of a sudden: fuzzy, furry, profoundly deep, as if he spoke from miles underground and it came up through the soles of their feet. Veris's heart hammered in sudden terror, and then anger: *Of course it wasn't him. Why didn't I see it?* She had so badly wanted to see the face of, if not a friend, someone she knew . . . *Nothing in here is as it seems. I have doomed us all with my trust.*

It was not him. It was someone more ancient, and more terrible, and Veris could not look at him as his disguise fell away like dust, and Eleonor screamed and buried her face in Veris's side. He became only a mountainous, indistinct shape, treetop-tall but also taller than that because deeper than that, buried in the ground of the forest, and buried in the clouds above the forest, further than mortal eye could see. She caught only a glimpse of the sharp recurved horns, the wide cloven hooves. She did not see eyes.

"And I know you lied," said the Lord of the Elmever, the great immortal god with no name, who had ruled this land before anyone had devised such a thing as names, and the voice went through her like an arrow and left her pierced and empty. "You lied . . . you did not pay your way here."

"I . . . no. I gave him my worst memory. As agreed."

"You did not. And now it is too late. You should have paid the price agreed the first time for the service rendered you. Now I choose another price. And it is him."

Veris's blood turned to quicksilver; she felt transfixed to the ground, rooted, as if she might never move again. Aram stood staring, shocked and unmoving, under the god's clawed and amber-leafed limb, his mouth open.

"No," Veris managed faintly, then put all her strength into her voice. "No, please. Take anything else from me. Years of my life, decades. Any memory. My name, my childhood. This is not his fault. He is innocent. I lied, me. Not him. *Not him!*"

"Innocence is no refuge," the god said, and reached out, scoring with his claw a line in the air that burned brightly for a moment, then tore like wet cloth, revealing a long grassy slope gleaming in the last rays of the sunset, and in the distance, the minuscule golden stars of the windows in the castle. Eleanor made a noise in her throat, but did not break her gaze from her brother.

"He is the price," the god repeated; and Veris was sure she felt her bones rattle inside her, shake against the flesh and the skin. All around she seemed to hear the forest listening, even praying: for their lord had made himself manifest and something long-hidden was hidden no more.

She gasped for air. "Please. Let me pay."

"You may leave him, and in exchange you two may go; that is one way. Or all three of you may stay, and become my servants for all time. Choose."

Three deaths: that was right in some way, but she could not bear it. She must break the three. What matter now, when all luck was gone. "Then take me instead. Not him. Let these two go, if you will only let two go through your way. Please." Her voice sounded so thin, it could barely pass through the rain to the god's ears; but she could not make it any stronger. Her strength was gone. "Let them go."

"You have been given your choice."

"Take me."

"You have been given your choice."

She forced herself to look at Aram: his face stunned, still disbelieving. It would have been better to not look, but also an act of cowardice. "I am sorry," she said.

"Veris?" whispered Aram.

"Believe me," she said, and took Eleonor's arm, the girl unresisting, numb, and she did not shed one tear until the torn portal had closed behind them and the child's last, despairing cry was all that she heard.

~

Veris swam out of the darkness already weeping, and for a moment only felt peace, for she did not remember why she wept. Then it returned to her, crashing down like the broken side of a mountain, burying her, and she screamed, and hammered her fists on the grass, and clawed it up in ruts, and when the scream ran out she sobbed as if her heart would break.

It was a long time before she looked around herself again, and rose from her knees, in agony, and still soaked through, and dizzy now; the sky arched above black and clear, not a single cloud, filled with such stars as might have comforted her on any other night, and half a moon exactly. The air was clean, and scented faintly with woodsmoke.

"Veris?"

She helped Eleonor up from the grass, pushed the hair off her face. "Are you all right?" she asked the child dully. "Are you hurt?"

"No, I'm not hurt."

They regarded each other for a moment, what little they could see in the night. "I have failed," Veris murmured, looking down at her scratched and bleeding hands, covered now with mud to the wrists. "I have . . . I brought out only one . . . of the Tyrant's children. I am already dead. Forfeited my life but also my family's . . . the entire village."

"Veris, no."

"You, you go back," Veris said, putting a hand on the girl's wet shoulder to push her up the slope. "Go, tell your father . . . no, I don't know what you must tell him. I will go back into the woods alone and . . ."

"No, they'll kill you this time for sure! They won't let you take a single step. I . . . I'll go back for him. One day." Eleonor took a long, shaky breath. "When I'm older. I'll go back and get him. You did this twice. Twice. Nobody's ever even done it once. Please. Let's just . . . let's go home."

"He will destroy my home, little one."

"I'll tell him," Eleonor whispered, and began to weep again. "I don't know what I'll tell him but I'll tell him. Please, Veris. Stay here. On this side. Don't go back in."

Side by side, unspeaking, they wandered and wove their way back up the grass, and the guards cried out in astonishment at their coming, and in moments the gray stone burst into gladness with torches and lanterns, and the stained glass danced to greet them like a fallen rainbow.

The Tyrant had not left his throne room; some of his wives, Veris did not know how many, nor how to distinguish them from the other noblewomen who might be hanging around the place, had also stayed, and slept heaped in the corners like the hunting dogs tethered before the great fireplace. And it was warm inside, with a strong crossbreeze from the open windows, and the warmth made Veris and Eleonor shiver as they were escorted inside.

Veris knelt at the proscribed distance as Eleonor ran for her father, and embraced him as if he were not a monster; and she felt nothing about her impending death, only warm air and her soaked sweater drying and felting on her skin.

"Where is my son?" the Tyrant said.

"He could not come with us," Eleonor said rapidly, seizing her father's arm in both hands. "Father. Listen to me. Please do not punish her. She is a hero, a warrior. *Kanunec ladoudir.* We were taken prisoner, they were going to sell us to a monster—there was no way to break Aram from the trap, you have to believe me, because I have never lied to you. But *I* will—"

He brushed her aside as if she were a butterfly that had landed upon him, and she cried out as she fell from the platform, caught by a gaggle of the court ladies awakened by the commotion. As the Tyrant closed upon her all Veris could think was that she hoped the girl's mother was among them. It would be terrible to have waited in here all day, unsummoned by news of your children's return. May she put her arms around her child, may she feel the burning cheek.

The Tyrant lifted Veris to her feet, and put a hand on

his sword; his face was stone, hard and white, and only his eyes moved and burned. "Chest or head?" he said.

"Head," said Veris.

He paused, still without expression. "You are ready for death?"

"I don't care anymore, my Lord. I truly do not. Because..." She glanced at Eleonor, who was scrabbling and fighting in catlike silence to escape the two women who held her. "It's my fault. I lied. The price of the forest was my worst memory; I told them the death of my father. It was not. It was only the worst until my own child died. The child I recovered from the woods fifteen years ago."

He continued to stare at her in silence. Veris listened to the fire crackle, then said, "Her name was Ingrahid. I was very young. It was an accident. With a friend... a soldier. We meant to marry, and quickly, when we knew. But he died in the war. He did not even know her. So when she went in there, I went in too. I got her back. I thought that was the hardest thing I had ever done in my life. More than her birth, when I was screaming and afraid, and I cried and I called out for my mother who was dead. More than my mother's death. More than my father's.

"Because we came home... and my daughter became ill, and two years later she died in my arms. That was the worst memory. Her death. *Hers.* I think perhaps I have been dead since then. I have never told anyone this before. No one. I think that was why I was even allowed into the forest after your children. My Lord, let me tell you they are brave and true. They too were heroes in there. Heroes and warriors. If you want my head in the place of your son, take it. I see what you have done to this valley and that you succeed at all things. As I have failed at all things."

She closed her eyes. In the darkness she saw Ingrahid's face: wracked with pain, unable to understand why it would not relent. Had it been the woods? Something else? Some terrible thing waiting to be passed down the family line? It did not matter. Veris had felt the tiny heart flutter to a stop, and everyone told her she must be grateful for it, that the pain was over, but she had not felt gratitude; she had wanted her child alive and with her for the rest of her life.

"Go home," the Tyrant said, so quietly she almost didn't hear him.

"My Lord?"

"Go home. The guards at the gate will find a carriage for you. Get out of my sight."

~

What remained of autumn wore away in long convalescence, and Veris spent much of it in a bed that her aunt and their neighbor built in front of the fireplace on the ground floor of the little house. The wound in her hip healed into an ugly purple scar like a rotten fruit; the one in her shoulder went bad, and Dr. Ervun came and cut it open and washed it out and bandaged it up again.

Veris was feverish and strange for many weeks after this procedure, and saw dark shadows beckoning her to join them from the corners of the room, but it passed, and soon she slept normally again, and only at night instead of all day, and she moved back up into her beloved attic, where she dreamt all winter of the god of the forest chasing her through the dense woods like a fleeing stag.

Without warning, and without attribution, food appeared at irregular intervals on their back doorstep, and those of her neighbors—unmarked sacks of wheat and rice, dried field peas, once a wicker basket of ham and sausage. Twice there were metal canisters of raisins and hazelnuts, and her aunt made spice-cakes for the solstice with them, and it seemed very strange to Veris to taste something so sweet in mid-winter. Clearly they were from the castle; and just as clearly, nothing could be said about it. Grandfather adored the canisters, and pilfered them from the kitchen to use in the garden, and he and her aunt had a week-long row about it.

And in the spring, on the first fine day, she left Grandfather sleeping late and went outside to let the rabbits out of their hutches, because there was grass now poking through the snow and some of them would want to stay in their cozily-made home and others would want the air and the green. As she did so, a small form walked up to the stone fence, and rapped upon it like a door, and Veris went over, wiping her hands on her apron.

"Good morning, Veris," said Eleonor.

"Good morning," Veris said. The girl wore what she probably thought of as a plain or unremarkable gown, thick brown velvet with a few tangles of golden leaves embroidered at wrist and throat, under a luxurious gray fur; her black hair was loose, and longer than the previous fall. In the road, the great steel-wheeled carriage, its four horses and driver, all were still and silvery as a statue in the early light.

Veris said, "Are you well?"

"Yes, I think so. And are you well?"

"Maybe I will be someday," Veris said. "Thank you for sending us food, by the way."

"What?"

Veris frowned; the girl seemed genuinely confused, and that confused Veris too. Who else could send it down without consequence so many times? There had been at least a dozen deliveries. Couldn't be one of the local boys recruited as a guard.

Then she shrugged, because it did not matter, and looked at the girl more closely, seeing the dark circles under her eyes. It would have been hard enough as a child of the Tyrant with only one true friend in the castle; Veris felt a great pity for her that she now had none. Her brother had surely been her shadow: ever-present, the most familiar thing in all that pile of gray stone, his face better known to her than her own. She would think about him at night and weep; and one day, Veris realized, she had wept her last, and made a decision.

Still, she said, "What brings you to our village?"

Eleonor looked around furtively; no one was out on the streets yet, although further down, in the village proper, there would be a few people around the bakery or the smithy, who had to start their fires early. "I'm ready to go back to . . . to the woods. That place in the woods. I spent all winter learning how to fence and ride with the guards; and to tie knots, and to throw knives, and all sorts of stuff. But now I want to learn from you," she said. "Magic. I want to learn how to do what you can do."

"Well, I don't know that it can be taught."

"But you don't know that it can't," the girl said, sensibly enough. "Please? At least I want to . . . make my own magical things. Like yours."

"I don't have mine anymore," Veris said. "I didn't get them back from Aram."

"All the more reason then," Eleonor said. "Don't you think? You can make new ones, maybe. We can make new ones together. And you can teach me. Will you?"

Veris pondered for a moment, then reached down and thumbed the latch of the garden gate. "I will think about it," she said. "Shut that tight behind you, please."

"You have so many rabbits!" Eleonor came in and stooped to pet them, laughing as they leapt away from her, careless of her fur; Veris grabbed it before it slid off her shoulders. "Do they all have names?"

"Not all. Just these two, because they are old, and they don't have kits anymore, and Grandfather won't let us eat them." Veris took the girl's elbow and raised her up, smiling for the first time in what felt like months. "Come in. I will tell you their names."

"And then you'll teach me magic?"

"No. Then we'll have a cup of tea. And then we will discuss what may and may not be learned."

Acknowledgments

As ever, I would like to thank Michael Curry, my dedicated and tireless agent. I also owe a great debt to the wonderful Tor folks who worked on this book with me, Jonathan Strahan and Eli Goldman, who truly understood what the story was getting at and never tried to knock it into a different shape or smother its idiosyncrasies. Finally, I would like to acknowledge our incredible cover artist, Andrew Davis, who so beautifully captured the spirit of this book.

About the Author

PREMEE MOHAMED is a multiple-award-nominated Indo-Caribbean scientist and speculative fiction author based in Edmonton, Alberta. She is an assistant editor at the short fiction audio venue *Escape Pod* and the author of the Beneath the Rising series and other works. She can be found on Twitter at @premeesaurus and on her website at www.premeemohamed.com.

TOR·COM

Science fiction. Fantasy. The universe.

And related subjects.

*

More than just a publisher's website, *Tor.com* is a venue for **original fiction, comics,** and **discussion** of the entire field of SF and fantasy, in all media and from all sources. Visit our site today—and join the conversation yourself.